Praise for John Cleveland

John Cleveland has written another winner! *Rural Royalty* compares and contrasts a rural couple from Idaho with a royal couple from the Kingdom of Taggart. They really aren't that different in their essence. This novel will draw you into the majesty of Idaho's mountain wilderness and her people, with a glimpse of the downside of being a "royal." Fantastic novel with real world personal issues. You have to read it!

SCOTT COTTRELL, AUTHOR OF *WHEN CHAOS REIGNS*

Steeped in Shaolin grabs you by the gi on page one and draws you through teenage brawls, secret emails, and kiss-in-the-park surprises faster than you can shout "hiya!" The author wields a black-belt gift for holding your attention while scattering valuable, relevant nuggets on courage, friendship, and faith like fortune cookies tossed into a whirlwind—snag one and you'll snap to the next page just to see what cracks open next. I couldn't put it down.

KYLE HILL, AUTHOR OF *THE BULLETPROOF AND UNBREAKABLE MARRIAGE*

Once again John Cleveland weaves a story full of adventure, mystery and his love of the great outdoors. *Rural Royalty* is a must read for anyone who enjoys a narrative that is both thought provoking and highly entertaining.

KATHLEEN ENGELBY, REVIEWER

Rural Royalty was another book written by John that I didn't want to put down. The characters coming from different backgrounds and the challenges they faced remind me that everyone carries burdens others can't see. I truly felt more grateful for the life God has given me after reading *Rural Royalty*.

BECKY MASON, REVIEWER

40 is a captivating compilation that blends timeless wisdom with contemporary storytelling, offering readers a profound journey through insightful narratives. Each parable, meticulously crafted by John, resonates with relevance to our modern lives while drawing from deep-rooted moral and philosophical underpinnings.

ANDY LEBLANC, REVIEWER

In this eclectic mix of stories, Cleveland gives Jesus' parables a modern twist, applying a range of genres and situations that resonate across a spectrum of interests and lived experiences. He presents biblical teachings in imaginative ways that are faithful to Scripture and always point back to Jesus. I can imagine these stories launching lively conversations with fellow believers and nonbelievers alike.

SARA BRUNSVOLD, AUTHOR OF *THE EXTRADORDINARY DEATHS OF MRS. KIP*

Rural Royalty

RURAL ROYALTY

John Cleveland

Published by JC Writing

Copyright © 2025 by John Cleveland

All rights reserved

No part of this book may be reproduced, or stored in a retrieval system, or transmitted in any form or by any means, electronic, mechanical, photocopying, recording, or otherwise, without express written permission of the publisher.

The characters and events portrayed in this book are fictitious. Any similarity to real persons, living or dead, is coincidental and not intended by the author.

ISBN-13: 979-8-9988931-3-1

Cover design by: M.G. Taylor
Printed in the United States of America

John Cleveland

This book is dedicated to Scott, who demonstrates with consistency what it means to be a husband, father and friend.

Rural Royalty

VIII

IX

Royalty consists not in vain pomp but in virtues.

-    Agesilaus II

Rural Royalty

x

INTRODUCTION

Royalty. Does simply coming out of a particular womb give one superiority over another? Does the blood of certain families have a premium quality, unlike the regular unleaded that flows through your veins?

When aristocracy comes to mind, we often think of aloof characters living in opulence, who flippantly give the order to imprison or even behead someone if their toast is burnt. Although that has existed in history and may still exist in certain parts of the world, some of our most visible samples of royalty have displayed qualities on the other end of the spectrum. They hold hands and smile at each other with obvious affection. They interact with normal people and often perform genuine acts of kindness. Their faces reflect sincerity and even humility considering their station. Even the smallest gestures form a connection to those of lower tiers who will never know the finer things in life.

I suppose that I can relate to their regal circumstances. By comparison to much of the world, I live in extreme luxury. Believe it or not, I have never opened a bare refrigerator. It's true. I actually have a knob on my bathroom wall that delivers hot water on demand. I can even fine tune it to my precise liking. Beyond this, I travel just for fun. I experience delicious meals that I did not cook. My clothing can be discarded when it no longer suits my taste. Lights can be left on without thought. My home can remain heated or cooled even when I'm not there. Thus, disparity exists above and below us all.

The purpose of this story is to contrast and compare two couples who are similar in age and character. Each has needs that feel very significant to them and has something specifically unique to offer others. There are moments of raw humanity that require grace and forgiveness. There is lavish generosity with things that cost money and with things that don't.

As you read about these couples, develop a mental picture of what they look like. Imagine their expressions and reactions to situations. Put yourself in their shoes and then take it one step further by walking in them. Regardless of your station in life, look around for opportunities to extend a hand downward to those just beneath you. Make a connection. Be royal even if you're not.

PROLOGUE

The Knight's Stoner KS-1 rifle was slung across the soldier's chest. The weapon's bolt was "in battery" with a 5.56x45mm NATO round seated in the chamber and the selector-switch was on "safe." A simple flick of the thumb and only 2.5 pounds of pressure on the trigger would send the firing pin forward, where it would strike the bullet's primer. In the confines of the chamber, the resulting explosion of gunpowder would send the projectile screaming down the spiral-grooved barrel at over 3,100 feet per second. In less than two seconds, it would be over a mile downrange. Whatever, or whoever, was in its path would be having a very bad day.

"I expected something like this from these dodgy blokes," the soldier spat with a rancorous Taggish accent.

His partner's mood was equally sour. "Bloody idiots. This will be the second greatest screwing the yanks have ever given us."

Their scowling faces continued to scan the nearby tree line. It had been a terrible assignment from the start. The preliminary op order called for a "backstage" presence: plain clothes, concealed weapons, zero confrontation. They had been acting more in the role of invisible babysitters rather than the elite soldiers they had trained for the better part of their adult lives to be. Only the worst of worse-case scenarios could justify any deviation from their commander's mandate. Twenty-four hours prior, it had happened.

Both men were using bravado to hide their inner turmoil. Fear causes many men to become rattled, but the source of their agitation was more akin to a bear protecting its young. If a person was behind this disappearance, no international law or agreement would protect that vile fiend from the extensive wrath they were capable of.

Suddenly, the radios attached to their chests began to squawk. The transmitted voice was shrill with excitement and equally Taggish.

"NORTH PERIMETER! SUSPECT SIGHTED! ALLEN, BAILEY, DO YOU COPY?!?"

Instinctively, both men snapped their rifles to a firing position and looked just over the sights with eyes wide open. In one more second, both men had acquired the target. Adrenaline, duty and anger signaled their leg muscles to fire as both men began to sprint toward the nearby trees. It would take them less than 15 seconds to cover the 100-yard gap, even with their equipment. In the milliseconds it took their minds to process the threat, they instantly knew that the rifles could not be used. The suspect held a female draped in his arms, possibly her.

Their VO2 max was quickly reached but it didn't matter. Whatever pain or discomfort this involved was inconsequential. A nation's fate rested on their shoulders.

"DROP THE GIRL! DROP HER!!!" they both shouted as they drew near. The suspect seemed dazed and was visibly staggering. Perhaps it was their verbal commands, or maybe the suspect's exhaustion, but the body in his arms fell to the ground like a sack of grain. One of the soldiers slung his rifle behind his back as he dove onto the fallen form. It was probably to shield her from the veritable explosion that took place a moment later.

The second soldier struck the suspect with everything he had, his shoulder spearing him solidly in the ribs. Any remaining wind was forced from the lungs as bones cracked. His feet left the ground as his body was flung backward from the blow of the human projectile. Thankfully, he was knocked unconscious, which spared him from the pummeling that accompanied his subdual.

Chapter 1

Territory of Idaho

August 1866

The only souvenir he had kept from the war was a slight limp. The surgeons had been unable to remove all of the musket ball's shrapnel but at least he'd been able to keep the leg. Not every man left that terrible conflict wholly intact. Fighting his own kind for the last four years had left even worse wounds in his mind. Acting as his own psychiatrist, he prescribed for himself a complete change of venue. With no surviving friends and no family to speak of, he had decided to head west.

During the war, it had become the soldiers' favorite pastime to talk about what they were going to do when it was finally over. Some were going home to their families' estates, perhaps to take up farming. Others wanted to move north to cities where manufacturing work was in demand.

Clyde Bardwell listened to all the other men's musings as he silently planned his own migration. Rumors of gold in the western territories were already spreading like wildfire, so he was not too keen on advertising his strategy.

A wagon, pair of mules, shovels, picks, pans, powder, fuse, bacon, lard...Clyde mentally prepared his packing list night after night as he tried to ignore the looming possibility of dying the next day.

Dreams have no value if you're dead.

Finally, the day had come when his uniform was no longer relevant. The rifle was no longer used to defend life by taking it. Released from his conscription, he could just...be.

The dust on the battlefield was still damp with blood as the ruts of his westward wagon appeared.

The months of travel had been precarious, liberating, exhausting, doubt inducing and entirely fulfilling. Having never been across the Mississippi River before, he marveled at the alien-like scenery that greeted him as he passed through what is now western Nebraska and southern Wyoming. Danger lurked in every form imaginable to include prairie fires, windstorms, desperately hungry pioneers and disease. However, they only served as confirmation that whatever treasures the West held were worth seeking. Nothing of real value comes easily. With an immunity to fear and perpetual gratitude for simply being alive, he forged westward with a dignified determination.

Perhaps his mules were following the scent of other animals. Or, maybe Clyde was guided by some magnetic attraction similar to that of a homing pigeon that can't help but to fly home. Whatever the reason, one day he called for the animals to "Whoa!" as he set the lever of his wagon brake. He had finally arrived where he wanted to live and die.

The Territory of Idaho was only populated by about ten thousand souls at the time. It may as well have been ten because he had not seen another human in over a month. He had pledged to himself to push beyond where the casual and complacent settlers might settle. As their wagons and homesteads developed along the level and accessible grounds, he pressed further into the wilderness. Mountains of green and granite loomed on the horizon and seemed to taunt him with their forbidding magnificence. He, in turn, accepted their challenge by penetrating deeply into their seclusive terrain. Isolating himself along the banks of the Salmon River, his search was over.

The first several weeks consisted of constructing a cabin, collecting wood for the winter and preserving meat. When at last he felt he had a sufficient margin of provision, he began to dip his cast iron pan into the clear, cold flowing waters. Unlike the muddy waters of the east, these were pristine and agreeable to the tastebuds.

Sometimes, he gazed open-mouthed, mesmerized at the sheer grandeur of his surroundings. Dense clusters of pines reached skyward and clung to the slopes until the steepness exceeded the grasp of their roots. As the elevations exceeded 10,000 feet, the rich dark soil of the lowlands could not attain the heights where only granite and limestone resided.

Gratefully, that first winter had been unseasonably mild. Warmer temperatures and dramatically less snow had made it unexpectedly tolerable. By spring, he'd harvested enough gold to finance the entire next year of operations. More importantly, his success served as fuel for his ingenuity. Just as he had done for so many nights beside those battlefield campfires, he continued to dream of his unique and unorthodox plans for the future.

As he left town with his newly purchased supplies, he carefully retraced and erased his steps back to his sanctuary of solitude.

The topography of the west is most unusual. It's as if at some point in history, when rock and mud were malleable, Mother Nature had used a giant stirring stick to twist and fold the layers like caramel. As they hardened, they maintained their contorted posture, which left the waters with no choice but to leap headfirst down the resulting chasms and cliffs. The wildness of Idaho would be difficult to discover and almost impossible to tame.

However, Clyde had found a bend in the Salmon that

he described to himself as "most advantageous." Some tectonic activity in the past had caused a colossal wedge of rock to slide into the path of the river, suddenly turning it north. If one were to explore just beyond the bank of the river, they would find that the elevation was below that of the water level. For millennia, the impromptu granite dam had held back the waters, which would have greatly desired to travel down the steep decline on the other side if the rock had only been susceptible to erosion. With powder keg and fuse in hand, Clyde intended to give it its wish.

Although he did not realize it, the Salmon River was lower than it had been in a century. It only took an afternoon of shoveling and moving small boulders until he had rerouted what was left of the flow. Instead of occupying the left channel against the cliff face, the water now veered right into a newly dug canal, leaving him with a dry area to work.

The next day, he bore a hole in the rock at a downward angle that he filled with powder and fuse. He sealed the opening, struck the flint and retreated to cover behind a nearby boulder.

Birds fled from the trees as the thunderous report shook the mountains. With over a twenty-mile buffer between him and the nearest human, he was not concerned with disrupting the neighbors. A large hole about three feet in diameter now permeated the surface of the rock. Clyde grinned as the substance of his dreams slowly became a reality. Over time, the blasting would continue until the borehole penetrated the massive granite wedge.

As the waters rose the following spring, the hole was completely submerged. The portion of the flow that was secretly diverted away from the main channel would be used to power a small but capable mill where the unification of gravity and water weight could be utilized. He now had the power of twenty mules at his disposal. Corn could be ground, rope could be pulled, rocks could be polished. Hidden in the recesses of the rocks, Clyde was now enjoying the benefits of Idaho's first and never-to-be-discovered hydropower plant.

Chapter 2

January 9, 1982

Penning, Taggart

Although David was not prone to being overly emotional, he felt a novel and unique sense of wonder as he stared at the tiny human being that his wife, Cynthia, had just delivered. She slept soundly in the hospital bed to his left. Having been married only a year and a half, they still qualified as newlyweds. This new addition only added to the sense of acceleration their lives now possessed.

I need to slow down and appreciate this moment, he thought to himself as he continued to gaze upon his darling little girl. *Who will she be? What will she do? Will she marry? If so, to whom? Will I like him? Will I approve?*

The "wills" continued to accumulate as he pondered the possibilities of her future. He supposed that a path of poor decisions could send her on a collision course with tragedy and hardship but, for reasons that he could not fully articulate, he felt that she was destined to walk a higher road. His brow furrowed in thought as he tried to imagine the years to come.

Chapter 3

April 25, 2002

Salmon, Idaho

The wedding was a very simple affair. It had to be. After all, the combined net worth of the bride and groom was just over $1,200. Adjusted for vehicle depreciation, credit card debt and a small pending fine at the library, it was closer to negative $1,820. Joey and Anna stood on the low stage of the Salmon Unity Chapel as the pastor asked the obligatory "do you?" and "do you?" The two were grinning like cheshire cats as he pronounced them husband and wife. They kissed, turned to the small assembly in the little church and bounded their way down the aisle before heading off to their honeymoon.

Well...actually, they were still saving up for their honeymoon. All they could afford tonight was dinner at the Rowdy Calf Café and a box of chocolates. The evening was sweet and simple but, most importantly, they were now officially Mr. and Mrs. Joseph Woodford. In their young, naïve minds, the future was full of promise and excitement. Eventually, there would be vacations to faraway places with strange names they couldn't pronounce. The language of the people would be gibberish in their ears and the local fare would appear inedible. They would sample the strange food offerings and secretly communicate to each other with their playful eyes asking *what in the world are we eating?!?*

As they drifted off to sleep, her head on his shoulder, they dreamed of all the adventures they would have together: Paris, Venice, Rio, Tokyo, Morwell…

Chapter 4

April 29, 2011

Morwell, Taggart

No one would argue that it was the wedding of the century. What could be done to make the day any more regal? The imposing stone columns of the Abbey rose and clasped hands together above the proud and prestigious attendees. Access to this sanctuary meant one of three things – you were either clergy, press or some manner of royalty. Even if your veins did not flow with royal blood, you were most certainly closely acquainted with someone whose did.

The atmosphere was dignified yet electric. For the past six months, all of Taggart (and a great portion of the world) was closely following every tidbit of relevant news or gossip. What would her dress look like? Would they be nervous? Would there be any family drama? But as the day unfolded, the fairytale took form and transpired into another triumphant moment for a family that had ruled in some form for over a thousand years.

Gracelyn, or Grace as she liked to be called, was trying her hardest to suppress her smile as she and Winston reentered the main chamber through the highly burnished doorway behind the elevated portion of the cathedral. The guests stood at reverent attention on both sides of the aisle as orchestral music accompanied their long procession toward the exit. Although dashing in the red coat of his royal uniform, Winston paled in comparison to the vision walking beside him that was a true-to-life princess.

As they slowly emerged from the entrance, celebratory bells competed with the roar of the awaiting crowds. They craned their necks for just a glance at who could someday be the future king and queen. The ornate carriage pulled by four majestic white horses stopped just before Taggart's newest couple boarded and took their seats. The crowds and bells continued with their cacophony as if the coalescence of new love and centuries old history demanded it. They obliged the adoring fans with polite waves and measured smiles. After all, royalty always had an image to maintain.

Chapter 5

April 29, 2011

Salmon, Idaho

DING!!! The microwave sounded that it had finished melting their evening meal into something that loosely resembled the plate of food displayed on the Famished Farmer frozen dinner packaging. The cardboard tray bent precariously as Anna pulled the steaming entrée from the metal box and then carefully removed the plastic film. Joey sat at the square piece of plastic with black folding legs that served as their dining room table.

Their home was as neat as it could be under the circumstances. You can only polish worn out linoleum countertops so much. Everywhere you looked, repair was needed. The windows had tape around the edges to lessen the draft as much as possible. The paneled walls testified to their origins way back in the late 60s. The mismatched appliances reflected the advancement of kitchen technology through the 80s and 90s but not beyond the year 2000.

He barely looked up as the wilted tray was placed in front of him. The day had been defeating. It was one of those days when you should have just pulled the covers over your head and stayed in bed. Despite your best efforts, nothing is going to go right. As a farrier, Joey was frequently the target of complaints whenever a horse threw a shoe or injured an ankle. Never mind that the recommended duration of horseshoes was only four to six weeks. With quiet resignation, he would tend to the almost mistreated animals who only received the minimal care when the meager finances of their owners permitted it.

Over their nine years of marriage, Anna had become accustomed to the silence. She knew that it was his way, like most men, of dealing with difficulty. Although it was foreign to her, she understood that within his mind was a whirlwind of challenges and solutions that he could only hope would deliver them from this existence and into the memorable world that he'd promised her almost a decade ago.

They were weary. Life had become a burdensome trudge through a never-ending swamp of bills, obligations, cancelled plans and dead-end dreams. Where they were in life was not where they were supposed to be.

"The bank wants the truck," he flatly stated without breaking his vacant stare at something beyond the table.

Anna slumped a little further, her face numbly registering yet another blow that life was dealing them.

"How much?" she asked with an equal absence of emotion.

"Six hundred and fifty. Two months past due plus a penalty. Frank said he couldn't waive it again."

Everyone knew everyone in Salmon. Frank had been friends with Joey's dad and secured the loan that financed this place back in the day. Strange how thirty years of payments had not yet secured a deed. Life just kept interrupting and foiling plans. When Joey's dad passed away, they inherited the house, which also included the mortgage. It's been said that the American dream has lots of strings attached and this dilapidated dwelling was no exception. In the past year, a window needed replacing, the bathtub drain became clogged almost weekly and the roof really needed some attention.

"What are we gonna do?" she asked rhetorically. It had been this way since day one of their marriage. It seemed as if some cosmic governing agency had forbidden their success in life. Both had always been hard workers but were beginning to wonder "what's the use?" It seemed like the people who cheated, stole or just received a government check were doing better than them, and with a lot less effort. Gone were the fantasies of visiting Bora Bora, the Caribbean and the Great Wall of China. Now, they would be happy if they could just pay the power bill on time.

He absentmindedly stirred his mashed potatoes with his fork as he rested his temple on his other fist.

"This stinks." It was rare for him to complain. He was generally the strong one, the optimistic one. As she would sometimes vent her fears and frustrations, he would listen sympathetically. He'd been a shoulder for her to cry on. Consistently, he'd been the one to reassure her that "things will work out" and to "just hang in there." This crack in his veneer was unsettling to them both.

An uneasy moment of silence passed between them. Neither was eating, nor did they want to. Suddenly, the house felt like it was shrinking. The whole town felt like it was shrinking. It felt like the air around them was slowly being replaced with an emptiness that threatened to snuff out the lingering spark of life. Not their actual heartbeats, but the inner part of you that can endure hard things because you know that a season of relief is coming. Lamentably, they could no longer discern that distant light at the end of the tunnel.

At that moment, something fell just inches away from Joey's nose and landed on his plate with a splat. Mashed potatoes and gravy splattered on his shirt and face. Although he was not in the mood for surprises, he examined the intrusive object. It was a large chunk of soggy sheetrock that had fallen from the ceiling. Silence continued for a moment as Anna cautiously and curiously waited to see her husband's reaction. People can be unpredictable when they're near their breaking point.

Then, Joey convulsed. Air tried to escape from his mouth. Was he choking? Anna's concern was quickly reaching a crescendo when a bellowing laugh emanated from his mouth. Then another. And then more. In another moment, they were both laughing without restraint. The tension that had almost crippled them was lifting and, for the moment, the darkness in their dining room was slightly diminished. He reached across and placed his hand on top of hers.

"It's gonna be alright, honey. We're gonna make it through this." Her Joey was back.

Chapter 6

January 1, 2012

Morwell, Taggart

Exhausted was an understatement. As her personal aide left the room, Grace collapsed in a chair and took what felt like her first full breath of the day. As she slumped, she exhaled slowly and kicked off her high heels. Her feet ached, her legs were tight and nothing sounded better than a warm bath at this moment. She knew she could ring a bell and some staff member would rush into the room to fulfill any and every need she might express, but even that felt exhausting at the moment.

Winston wasn't faring any better. The last two weeks had been a marathon of Christmas galas, fundraisers, visits to orphanages, wrapping gifts for children, smiling, waving, more smiling all under the watchful and scrutinizing eye of the press. Last night's appearances and obligations had kept them out well past midnight and

New Year's Day had begun at 6:00am with another full itinerary. At the moment, they both looked stunningly undignified.

"I've never been so tired," she murmured to herself as much as to him.

With his chin resting on his chest, he only had the strength to raise his eyes to acknowledge her.

"Has it always been this way, Win?" she asked.

He furrowed his brow and thought about it. "I don't suppose I've ever known anything different. Mother was the queen of sociality. Come to think of it, I've never known the sort of Christmas where one would run down the stairs, tear open a trunk full of toys and spend the day just lounging about." His gaze became distant as he imagined such a life of leisure. "You become accustomed to it, I suppose."

This was not comforting to her. She'd been "serving" in this position for less than eight months and her seemingly endless stamina was fueled by some hope that things would soon abate. She expected the new to wear off and the public's attention to wane. Thinking about it now, things only seemed to be intensifying. There was no privacy. There was no down time. How was one supposed to rule a country if they didn't have the time for basic self-care?

"I'm not sure I can do this," she admitted with a tinge of fear in her voice.

Winston rose slightly in his chair. "Are you being

serious, Grace? Are you quite alright?"

She sat in silence as she recollected the past several months, weeks and days. They were all a blur of handshakes, curtsies, camera flashes, interviews, more photos, more smiles, "Remember your posture! Present yourself as royalty! The public needs to see you leading!" A wave of anxiety crashed over her already sapped soul.

Winston sat up even more and sharpened his attention toward her cheek. "Grace, are you...crying?" In a flash, he was on his feet, moving quickly to her side. He knelt beside her and slid his arms around her. He pulled her close as he felt her quiet sobs of breath and warm tears on his neck. He loved her now more than ever. She'd been so strong and had truly given everything to match the maddening pace of this train ride since they'd said "I do."

As he gently rubbed her back, he offered words of consolation that he knew would require action to be true. "Everything will turn out, my love. I promise."

Chapter 7

January 1, 2012

Evansville, Indiana

She waited in the park near the flower gardens. One would have thought that it was unsafe for her to be there alone after dark, but further inspection of her outfit would have insinuated that she was a woman of this particular time of day. Her fishnet stockings, leather skirt, low cut blouse and heavy makeup comprised the customary uniform of the world's oldest profession. She tapped the toe of her platform heel on the concrete sidewalk, casually scanning the area as if she was waiting for someone.

Her phone buzzed and lit up, indicating that a message had just been received. She read it, typed in a reply and continued to wait. In less than two minutes, a man appeared around the corner. He was dressed in slacks and a button up. Expensive leather shoes made faint knocking sounds on the ground as he approached.

He looked out of place here, especially at this time of night and especially with her. She smiled playfully as he drew near, twirling her hair with her free hand. He looked around furtively as if making sure the coast was clear.

"Why did you call me here?" he demanded with a hissed whisper.

Her smile became sly as she touched his shirt near the collar and let her hand slide down his chest. "You were a lot nicer to me on Sunday. Where is that guy? That's the guy I wanted to see tonight."

He swatted her hand away and looked around again in all directions. "This is not appropriate at all. I assumed you needed help when you contacted me. And you weren't dressed like this on Sunday. And you definitely weren't acting like this on Sunday."

She turned up the intensity of her exhibited attraction by placing her hands around his neck and pulling her toward him.

"What are you doing?!?" He wanted to push her away but couldn't find a polite place to put his hands on her. Their embrace became awkward and they danced around like two drunken winos. As he tried to move backward out of her embrace, she followed him as their feet became entangled. They rotated one hundred eighty degrees so that he was now trying not to fall on top of her.

Without warning, blinding lights erupted from the nearby hedges. Through the glare, he could make out two or three people holding objects out in front their bodies as they approached. They said nothing as they stopped about ten feet away.

They're filming! he realized with horror.

"This is not what it looks like! I am not with this woman!" he shouted as they continued their entangled tango around the shadowed solitary space. Instantly, she looked shy and embarrassed. She peeled away from him and covered herself with her arms as if her clothes had suddenly disappeared.

He stood there with open arms, palms up and a bewildered expression on his face. His mind was quickly connecting the dots. His recent separation from his wife, the distraught young lady pleading for his counsel, the late-night desperate phone call. It felt as if he'd fallen, or rather been pushed, into a swimming pool of evil.

In tense situations, the mind goes into overdrive and processes at a much higher level than at any moment during a banal day. He thought about the multiple ministers he'd known through the years who had been caught up in scandals. His mind recalled images of them crying from their pulpits, pleading with the congregation and God to forgive them. If absolution happened, it wasn't visible. Their confession was always the last step before their resignation or termination.

Now, his church – his baby that he had carefully and methodically raised since its infancy was suddenly receding into the distance like a kidnapped child. *How could this have happened?* he pondered. And more profoundly, *why is this happening?*

Chapter 8

January 2, 2012

Salmon, Idaho

Scott Olens looked down at his phone to see who was texting. It was his brother, Jacob, who lived and worked in Manhattan.

Incoming: HAVE YOU SEEN THE NEWS TODAY? ANOTHER ONE BITES THE DUST! GOD BLESS HIS SOUL. (LAUGHING EMOJI WITH PRAYER HANDS)

Scott's stomach sank as he clicked the attached link. It was a video clip from a popular tabloid website, Exposed HD. As it began to play, it showed the nationally recognizable Pastor Mark DuBois struggling with who appeared to be a prostitute. He was stumbling in the glare of the lights, his arms groping the provocatively dressed lady who somehow looked very much like a completely innocent victim in that moment. The pastor turned toward the camera with a shocked expression as he exclaimed, "This is not what it looks like! I am not with this woman!"

It looked bad. His knee jerk reaction was bitter disappointment that all things Christian or church-related were receiving yet another black eye. He felt resentment toward this pastor who ostensibly had been living a double life, preaching one thing from the pulpit but privately practicing something entirely different. A small part of his mind wanted to believe that it was all a misunderstanding. Maybe he had an evil twin? Maybe the girl was his niece? He shook away the foolish self-delusions.

His brother had allowed enough time for him to watch the clip before he launched his next volley.

Incoming: YOU BETTER NOT LET ME CATCH YOU IN THE PARK WITH SOME HOOKER. NO SENSE IN BOTH OF US TARNISHING OUR FAMILY'S REPUTATION.

Needless to say, his brother's sense of humor lacked any sense of decorum. He loved Jacob. He prayed for Jacob. He tried to have a relationship with his brother but there was always some invisible barrier preventing it. If Scott was being kind, he was being pious. If he expressed concern, he was being judgmental. If he gave space and didn't pursue a relationship, he was being even more judgmental. It was a no-win situation that played on his mind continually.

Something is sabotaging us, was his ultimate conclusion. It was the only way to reconcile the negative reception to his efforts of being kind. He looked back at his phone and saw the frozen image of Mark DuBois' horrified face hidden behind a "play" icon. Out of curiosity, he pressed the screen to continue the clip. A booming voice accompanied by heavy metal guitar riffs spoke over the clip:

"ANOTHER FRAUD EXPOSED, HD STYLE, STYLE, style, style, style!!! YOU MIGHT HAVE FOOLED YOUR CONGREGATION BUT YOU'RE NOT FOOLING US, US, us, us, us." The voice was deep, raspy and had globs of added reverb like you'd hear at the Grand Canyon. Scott slumped back on his sofa and let the cloud of discouragement that was seemingly transmitted through the phone envelop him.

Chapter 9

February 14, 2012

Salmon, Idaho

The Sip-N-Shake drive-in diner was almost deserted on this Tuesday Valentine's Day, and with good reason. Burgers and fries did not convey romance the same way that gourmet entrees and candlelight do. Sadly, Salmon did not offer this option. Even if it had, Joey and Anna could have only afforded two waters and an appetizer. Even if you wanted the experience of a nice restaurant, you couldn't escape the disapproving frown of your waiter. No server is ever excited about getting 15% gratuity of an $8.99 order.

They sat in their 1995 Chrysler Minivan. She had borrowed it from her mother after the truck had been repossessed. Her family had done an impressive job of keeping the aging vehicle in surprisingly good shape. However, the daily transport of farrier tools and home repair material was having a very visible effect. They would have to deal with that challenge in the future.

Sucking on his straw, Joey was silent as he tried to extract the thick, chocolatey mixture. He'd been increasingly quiet for the last several weeks. Anna couldn't help but wonder if his discontentment with life extended to their marriage. She was still attractive and helpful. She tried to be upbeat and supportive, except for the frequent lapses when she just didn't have it in her to pretend. She continued to work at the Sprout School daycare making just over minimum wage, but her financial contribution to the family felt like bailing water from the Titanic with a single bucket.

She knew bringing up their circumstances would ruin yet another Valentine's Day. She knew that he interpreted her voiced concerns as complaints about his performance as a provider and a husband. It was a no-win situation. She needed to talk. She needed to vent her anxieties. But not tonight. She took her Styrofoam cup and took another sip of her shake. Since it was a "special" night, she chose strawberry.

Chapter 10

March 2, 2012

Morwell, Taggart

Please, Winston. No more today," Grace pleaded as the door to their Land Rover was shut by a royal guardsman.

He looked slightly frustrated. "You know that's not possible."

She countered, "Win, I am dreadfully weary. This pace never ends! I know you care about the people and your duties, but what about your duty to me?"

He turned and examined her as he tried to discern if she was being intentionally offensive or merely expressing a desire to be close to him. He opted for the latter.

"Grace, you have been quite the consul and I promise that we shall have our holiday. It's already in the works." He inwardly flinched knowing that "already in the works" only meant that'd he'd intended to look into it soon. Half-truths are very close to lies.

Her face lit up at his comment. "Really? This sounds promising. Where are you thinking about?"

He smiled to camouflage the twinge of guilt he felt and looked outside of the moving vehicle for some divine inspiration. He needed to give an answer, and quickly! He then noticed a billboard that was advertising a new all-natural grocery store. The picture displayed a steaming potato that had been split open and was chock full of vegetables and bits of meat.

"Idaho!" he exclaimed. "We are going to...Idaho." His forced smile remained as he nodded to himself and averted his eyes.

"Idaho? As in, the United States? What on earth shall we be doing in Idaho?" She added incredulous emphasis to the last word.

He had gone too far to back down now. "What? Are you serious? Everyone wants to go to Idaho. It's been on the top 10 list for adventures, oh, I'd say for the last several years. It has...mountains and...rivers and...potatoes." He gave her his best playful smile, which had the desired effect. She was genuinely interested in his impromptu escapade. The foul mood had passed and she was enthusiastic once again. Her smile was the reward he was seeking and it had its desired effect as well.

Although raised in privilege beyond comparison, Winston had innately avoided taking full advantage of the lavishness that his position afforded. However, there were occasions that merited pulling rank and using resources. He determined his course of action on the spot and silently reassured himself. *I am the Duke of Ulbridge and Grace is my wife. I will see this done.* He looked out of the window. *Idaho, please be exciting.*

Chapter 11
March 31, 2012
Salmon, Idaho

cott arrived at the Traveler's Ranch that afternoon. As the town's only large animal veterinarian, his work consisted mostly of house calls. Bringing your sick horse or cow down to the clinic obviously posed some challenges. His Ford F-250 4X4 bounced down the muddy driveway toward the barn where he noticed Joey's (borrowed) minivan. Inwardly, he perked up at the thought of seeing his friend. For some reason, Joey had been on his mind lately and he'd been wanting to check in with him. Outwardly, he frowned at the absence of Joey's work truck. In such a small town as Salmon, even news of the repossession and its associated gossip made its rounds.

He grabbed his medical bag and made his way to the large, sliding barn door. As he pushed it open, there was Joey sitting on his customary three-legged wooden stool with a horse's hoof nestled in his arm. With the other, he was digging out mud and dirt and anything else that a horse could pick up on the trail.

He looked up. "Hey, Scott. How's it goin'?" His tone was dull.

Scott smiled warmly as he greeted his friend. "Hey, bud. Another day, another dollar."

Neither was effusive with their dialogue but that was OK. True friendship is dependent on trust and presence rather than shallow words. Scott made his way to one of the stalls and opened his bag as he began his examination of a quarter horse that had apparently lost its appetite.

"You guys been doin' OK? How's Anna?"

Joey paused for just a bit too long. "We're alright...I guess. The winter has been a little slower than I'd like."

"Always is. But that's what makes the coming of springtime all the better." Scott was an incurable optimist. Joey didn't reciprocate the question and silence ensued. Scott was moving his stethoscope around the horse's side and belly as he listened through the earpieces. *Everything sounds clear. Need to check the mouth*, he thought as he moved around to the front of the animal.

"Sorry about the truck," he blurted out without thinking.

The sound of scraping from the other stall stopped. The silence deepened.

"My bad, Joey. It's gotta be a sore subject."

More silence.

Scott stood there uncertain as to what he should do. With men, you need to be careful how much concern you show. With a strong man, you are in danger of insulting him. Curiosity got the better of him and he moved around the petition to make sure Joey was still there. As he did, he saw Joey still holding the horse's leg in one arm and the metal pick in the other. He was staring ahead catatonically. "You alright, bud?"

Joey blinked and then slowly redirected his gaze at Scott. He looked like a shell-shocked soldier fresh from the battlefield. Scott moved in and took a knee a few feet away from the other man. Joey opened his mouth to speak but no words came out. He looked searchingly at Scott but nothing was found to loosen his tongue.

Scott knew to proceed with caution. "It's alright, bud," was all he said. He looked down at the ground so as not to embarrass his friend.

"I'm drowning, man," Joey finally admitted. "The truck, the bills, the house. Everything is just...piling on top of me like an avalanche. I can't dig out fast enough. Anna's not happy. I'm not happy. We're just like two robots going through the motions, day after day. It's not what I promised her. Man, I just..." The words caught in his throat as he paused to assemble his thoughts. "It's just not working. I feel like there's some evil wizard out there that's put a curse on us and I don't know why and I don't know how to break it."

Truer than you think, Scott thought to himself. He remained quiet as Joey continued.

"Man, I just don't know what to do. If I work harder and make more money, it just means that more things break and need fixin'. If I make plans with Anna, it's just a surefire way to make sure something comes along to screw 'em up." With that, he threw down the pick into the straw and covered his face with his hands as he tilted his head back. Through his fingers, the anguish was obvious. "My God! If You're up there, what in the world are you up to?!?"

It wasn't exactly a prayer, but all conversations need to start somewhere. Scott knew that Joey was not particularly spiritual. He was definitely not a man of faith. But he was a good man. He was faithful – to his wife and to his word. If you had car trouble on a cold, rainy night, just a phone call to Joey and he'd be there to help, even if he had to walk or crawl. He could keep a secret. He didn't gossip and seldom complained. But every man has his breaking point. It looked like Joey was nearing his. *This could be a good thing*, Scott thought. He silently prayed for wisdom before he spoke.

"I'm sorry, man. That sounds tough." It wasn't very philosophical or theological, but it was heartfelt and compassionate.

Joey nodded that it was appreciated. "She just deserves better than this. It's killing me not to be able to give it to her." He paused. "Maybe she needs to be with somebody else."

Too far. Time to speak up. "That's not the answer, Joey. You two need to stick together. You *are* going to stick together. You're gonna get through this. You can't see it right now, but this is making you stronger." He paused as he formed his next words and prayed again not to say anything damaging. Suddenly, it came to him.

"Do you know what a Misogi is?"

Joey looked at him questioningly.

"It's something the Japanese Samurai used to do. They would go out in the wintertime and stand under a waterfall as a way of purifying themselves. It helped them to push their limits and gain fortitude. They believed it gave them a better mental picture of their circumstances and helped them deal with whatever they were facing."

Joey was quiet. "So...you think I should go to Japan?"

A quick laugh escaped from his mouth. "That's funny. No, you don't have to go to Japan but let me ask you, when was the last time you went out by yourself into the woods?"

Joey thought about it and answered. "I don't know. I guess right after high school, before I started working full time. Life just got busy."

"Exactly! Too busy. Man, I know you're giving 110% right now but I think you need to spend a little time on yourself, get your head straight. You can't take care of anything or anybody if you're not doin' alright."

Joey mulled over this in his mind. It made sense but

it was completely contrary to the American way. You work hard. You don't take vacation days. You still go in even when you're sick. Someday, hopefully, you finally get ahead.

Scott must have been reading his thoughts. "How's that working out for you?"

Joey sat on the stool considering his friend's advice. One by one, the excuses were disappearing. "What about Anna?"

"Talk to her. She's your wife. Explain to her what you want for her, for the both of you."

"What about the horses? I'm the only farrier in town."

Scott smiled. The tension had eased enough to inject a little bit of humor. "Yup. Salmon will close its doors and go belly up if you go missing for a few days. We might ought to call the governor before all of Idaho shuts down."

Joey grinned for the first time in a long time. Scott continued, "I'll catch your calls while you're gone. You're not the only one who can shoe a horse."

Chapter 12

April 5, 2012

Salmon, Idaho

We need to talk." Joey's words hung in the air as he set his dirty dishes into the sink.

Anna froze in place as her eyes went wide. Her heart almost stopped with the recognition that this moment could be the execution of her fears that had been culminating for the last several months. She knew her husband wasn't doing well. She knew he was frustrated, restless and discontent. She also felt the wake of these emotions rolling over their marriage. A barrage of uninvited thoughts burst into her mind. *We didn't even make it to ten years. Ten years of my life! Were these the best years of my life? Has it all been wasted? What about my future? Do I even have one?*

Her gut twisted into a knot as she steeled herself and turned toward him. She tried to mask her vulnerability. Joey put his hands on the edges of the sink, the weight of the world bearing down on his shoulders. Visually, she noted his calloused and permanently stained hands. They were that way for them.

"Something's gotta give." His words were simple and raw. Whatever came next would be unfiltered and straight from his soul. "I think I'm broken."

The vise on her heart released its grip ever so slightly. She quickly walked to his side, placing one hand on his forearm and the other on his back. The essential physical contact was there but he still had space. His mouth hung open as he tried to continue.

"I just...can't keep going. I can't go on fighting to pay the bills, keepin' this dump from falling in on our heads..." he paused, "...letting you down." He turned his head away and gripped the sink edges even harder. A single syllable of sorrow escaped from his tightened throat before he cinched down hard on his emotions. Sustained strain for this long would break the hardest of men.

She moved in closer, pushing her chest against his side. She leaned her head on his shoulder. She felt the energy of his tension in her cheek as it transferred into her. This is what loving spouses do.

He sucked in a breath and blew it out slowly, still unable to face her. When enough moments had passed, she gently guided him toward the couch where they sat down, her embrace remaining intact. He sat there looking vacantly across their shoddy living room. The dingy brown paneling, the cheap cowboy art on the walls and the wilting ceiling fan blades all coalesced to reinforce the melancholy mood.

"I think I need to go away for a while."

Anna remained quiet as she continued to suppress the fears leaping up from their dark hiding places.

"Scott was telling me that I need to get alone, get away from..." he motioned toward the room with his hands, "...all of this." At this moment, Joey realized that his wife could easily be considering herself to be part of "all of this." For the first time this evening, he looked at her and locked eyes. "This is not your fault. You mean everything to me." His voice started to break as his eyes closed tightly. "It just hurts me so bad to know that I can't give you..."

She began to rub his back as it heaved under closely guarded sobs. He wrapped his arms around her and the release valve finally opened. In ten years, she'd never seen this side of him. Not when his dad died and not even when he'd accidentally shot himself through the hand with a nail gun. Emotions weren't his thing. It's what she'd liked about him. He was solid. Tough. Dependable. Maybe it came at the expense of romance and sweet sentiments but there were many ways to show those things. This was something new.

They sat there for maybe thirty minutes. Neither was in a hurry to move. She continued to rub his back. She waited quietly. She was there for him. Finally, he composed himself and looked back at his wife. The question hung in the air between them. *Where do we go from here?*

"You should go," Anna said as she looked down. "You work so hard for us and I feel it too. Something's gotta give. You need to go for you, and you need to go for us." They fell into each other and held each other. For tonight, this was more than enough. It was actually exactly what they needed.

Chapter 13

April 25, 2012

Morwell, Taggart

What do you mean, 'They've gone?'" the queen inquired of Bancroft, her aide.

"Ma'am, Winston has taken Grace on holiday. He said he wanted it to be a surprise for their first anniversary."

Confusion swept across the queen's face. "A surprise? How dreadful. How on earth did we produce such an impetuous boy? Is he ever going to take his responsibilities seriously?" She raised a hand to her forehead in a rare display of dismay.

Bancroft smiled. The moments of humanity he saw in her highness only made her more endearing. The years of faithful service gave him more liberty in both conversation and observation than most.

"We both know that is far from the truth," he gently declared. They both recognized that Winston and his new bride had been a much-needed boost for Taggart. For an often-dreary country, their visible joy and love for life had been a continual stream of light and hope.

"But what of their appointments? Their obligations? We have appearances to maintain, you know."

"Yes ma'am. We have arranged their schedules." He pronounced it with the proper *shed* as opposed to the barbaric western *sked*. "The media has been downright giddy in their quest for information about their escapade. Of course, Winston has demanded that their destination and itinerary be given the utmost discretion."

The queen nodded her acceptance of this stipulation. "Of course. Even royalty must protect the privilege of privacy." She pronounced her final word with a short "i" so that it sounded almost like *privilege*. Only a yank (or a pirate) would use a long "i."

"Bancroft, where are they going?" she asked him directly.

Her loyal servant pursed his lips and turned his gaze away toward the ceiling.

Her mouth dropped open in shock. "Bancroft! You will tell me this instant! Where have Winston and Grace disappeared to?"

"I'm sorry, ma'am. I've given my word."

And that was that.

Chapter 14
April 25, 2012
Chicago, IL

Chester Hannigan's hands danced over the keys and controls of the technical console. He sat in a modern leather office chair as he stared up at multiple screens.

It's all in the editing, he slyly thought to himself. With a little cut here and a little paste there, statements could be taken out of context, conversations could end in a brief moment of anger, and a facial expression that lasted but a second could be frozen in time.

He tapped a control into the keyboard and used the roller ball to zoom in on the subject. He was a modest looking man who appeared to be currently disturbed. The man's name was Michael Martin, also known as "The Saint." He was the founder and director of HeartSend, one of the largest non-profits in the United States. Seldom did an evening go by without a television viewer seeing him in one of their advertisements. Their heart-tugging scenes would show distraught and dirty people with eyes full of sadness staring into the camera as Michael's voice tenderly appealed in the voiceover.

"Your dollar a day can make the difference between life and death. Imagine if you had a child or loved one that could have been saved if someone, maybe even you, had just offered the change in their pockets."

Give me a break, Chester would think each time the commercial would interrupt his Monday night viewing of "Cheaters and Liars – The World's Greatest Con Artists." Unlike Michael Martin, they were truly deserving of hero status – men and women who knew how to work the system, find the loopholes and look out for number one.

His attention returned to the work at hand. The video showed Michael getting into a very expensive-looking Mercedes coupe. He was wearing a suit but had neglected to put on sunglasses. He appeared to be deep in thought as he pulled out of the rental lot and onto the street. Someone had apparently slowed down and motioned him into traffic, because he suddenly smiled brightly and shot a hand up in a friendly gesture. Chester tapped the keyboard again, which froze the image. A little trim on the front end of the clip. Now, the five second clip showed the benevolent icon glowering in the driver's seat of a luxury automobile and then flashing a madcap smile almost directly into the hidden camera. Just like that, the edited clip made him look completely superficial and materialistic. This manufactured image was obviously not aligned with what the ocean of HeartSend donors perceived in their minds.

Setting this up had been easy. A lone cameraman had set up discreetly across the street. His camera had been hastily camouflaged inside of a paper bag that was lodged into a row on low bushes. He had then given the twenty-year-old rental car agent a $100 bill with the agreement that no economy cars would be available when Mr. Martin arrived at the counter. As his target arrived to pick up his rental, he was puzzled and even disturbed by the unexpected "upgrade." Almost scornfully, he accepted the keys and sulked off to the lot. The rest was all captured on film.

It was the last clip in a series for this week's edition of Exposed-HD. Work like this took patience and cunning. In Chester's mind, these guys were all charlatans. He had already decided that the executive staff of these so-called benevolent organizations were playing on the sympathies of so many bleeding hearts. Sure, they would throw a small percentage of the proceeds toward some highly visible need and then the rest would be used for corporate retreats in the Bahamas and country club memberships. He stewed as he ruminated over this speculated corruption. *Alright, Michael Martin. Let's see how many people donate to you after this!*

Chapter 15

April 27, 2012

Salmon, Idaho

Scott Olens had finally reached the last page of the CEU on his laptop when his cell phone made a singular ding. He looked down and frowned as he saw Jacob's name as the sender. He had come to expect only critical communication from his brother, who seemed determined to bash anyone who exhibited any kind of light. Of course, his ire was always veiled behind some witty or sarcastic comment.

LOOK WHO'S BEEN STEALING COOKIES FROM THE COOKIE JAR!

There was a link to the website Exposed-HD. Not only did he need to finish his continuing education unit, but he dreaded seeing which esteemed public figure was about to be drug through the mud.

As dread filled his stomach, he pressed play. The video showed a segment of the familiar HeartSend commercial appealing to potential donors. Then, the footage switched to a conference where Michael Martin was describing how money was being distributed to desperate families and individuals around the world. Another clip of him leaving church with his family, a large bible tucked under one arm with his surprisingly attractive wife holding on to his other.

Suddenly, there was a clip of him putting on sunglasses and looking around as if he were being followed. Another clip showed him putting an envelope into the inner pocket of his suit jacket. In the next, he was sinking a putt at a golf course and then pulling a clinched fist to his side in a show of victory. A telephoto shot captured him cutting a piece of what appeared to be steak in a fairly nice restaurant and then rolling his eyes in delight as he masticated the meat. Lastly, there was the shot of him grinning manically at the camera as he pulled onto the street in a beautiful Mercedes-Benz CL-class.

None of these scenes individually conveyed any nefarious activity. However, their combined insinuations were more than enough to cast serious doubt as to the integrity of this organization and its leader. The booming stadium voice accompanied by the heavy metal music began to speak.

"DO YOU REALLY WANT TO SEND A DOLLAR A DAY TO THIS MAN, man, man? THAT'S THREE HUNDRED SIXTY-FIVE DOLLARS A YEAR AND IN THREE YEARS, IT WIN BE OVER A THOUSAND,

thousand, thousand. OR YOU CAN KEEP WASTING YOUR HARD-EARNED DOUGH dough dough. I'VE HEARD HE'S BEEN LOOKING AT A PRIVATE JET, jet, jet."

The image of Michael Martin zoomed into his smile and began to spin on the screen which disappeared into a rainstorm of dollar signs.

His brother, once again, timed his response to allow for the video clip to end.

DIDN'T YOU SEND THIS BOZO SOME MONEY? DIDN'T HE SEND YOU A CALENDER OR SOMETHING? SOUNDS LIKE A GREAT DEAL! (dollar sign and flame emojis)

Scott slumped back in his chair as he tried to come up with some witty comeback. Nothing came to mind and, if he was being honest, the video looked pretty incriminating. He made a mental note to look at his bank account to see if any money was being drafted for HeartSend.

Chapter 16
April 28, 2012
Yellowstone National Park, Wyoming

The small army of park rangers stood at the temporary barricades that had been erected at each of the walkways leading toward Old Faithful. Seas of disgruntled tourists badgered them with questions.

"Is it broken?" "Did somebody fall in?" "Will the body shoot up into the sky?"

One rather large and burly ranger suppressed an eye roll and tried to remain professional. "Sorry, folks. The next eruption will take place at approximately 4:15. The area is temporary closed for safety reasons."

Although this explanation did little to assuage the angry mob, a much smaller group of tourists with a front row seat to the geyser were witnessing one of nature's wonders. Grace's face radiated with joy as the sulphureous mist landed on her face. Nearby, Old Faithful hissed and gurgled like some limestone giant with indigestion. She leaned against Winston, who returned her smile and pulled her close with his arm around her shoulder.

The last few days had been nothing less than magical. Mind you, the average tourist would never have exclusive viewing rights of national landmarks, but some impressive credentials and a small unit of Taggish guards could make the impossible happen. There had been the private dining at the Four Seasons Lodge in Jackson Hole, the private photo shoot at the Antler Arch, the helicopter tour of the Grand Tetons and fly-fishing expedition down the Snake River. Grace had been thrilled at each new experience.

Of course, locals scratched their heads as crowds were evacuated and police tape was quickly strung up around popular attractions. Royalty had its privileges. Today's auto tour of Yellowstone was fascinating as they wound through the bizarrely beautiful intersection of Wyoming, Idaho and Montana. Winston was glowing as he observed his wife's visible glee and satisfaction.

"How on earth are we going to top today's adventure?" Grace asked as she squeezed Winston's arm. Playfully, he replied, "Oh, this? This is actually just the warm-up. I hope you're ready for some genuine excitement tomorrow." She blushed with joy and kissed him on the cheek. They were drunk on the delight of being newlyweds in a place that was very exotic by their standards. With a golden ticket to the best of America, their small motorcade exited the park near West Yellowstone and made its way west toward Salmon.

Chapter 17

April 28, 2012

Salmon River Mountain Range

I could get used to this, thought Joey as he stoked the fire and flipped his venison steak on the small portable grill. He hadn't been alone in the woods since he was a teenager, and their familiar bond was beginning to reacquaint. This was the third day of his solo expedition and he stifled the thought that he would have to return to the real world in two more. He hadn't uttered a word since greeting another hiker at the trailhead last Friday. With each passing hour, the sounds of nature had lost their shyness and fell pleasantly on his exhausted ears. Even now, the crackle of the fire, the clicking of branches blowing in the breeze and the distant hooting of an owl provided a therapy that no human counselor could.

He'd also had time to think without distraction. Like any typical man, he problem-solved by brooding. He decided to prioritize the things in his life so that if he had to begin cutting, only the most important would remain. Anna was number one. Even now, he missed her. Her sweet face, beautiful with or without makeup, floated in his thoughts. Since falling apart in front of her, they'd experienced a strange sense of closeness that somehow unified them in their fight against the drudgeries of life.

Number two was Idaho. He loved the land and deeply regretted letting the last ten years slip by without taking more advantage of this recreational wonderland that he called home. *How much does it cost to sleep outside?* he asked himself. He decided that he and Anna would make time to get some fresh air and go exploring at least once a week.

Number three was strange because it was an incomplete asset. His friends. Sure, there was Scott. They hadn't intentionally hung out since high school, but he always enjoyed bumping into him around town. There was Hank down at the hardware store. On second thought, he couldn't imagine actually hanging out with Hank. He was just a familiar face. It just seemed logical that he and Anna should each have some buds or peeps or whatever buzz words people were using these days. What about Anna? Did she have any true friends? Had he somehow inadvertently isolated her socially? A fresh pang of guilt filled his chest.

It had been this way for the last three days. Relief from the daily grind, dreams of a better life, guilt that he hadn't been able to give it to Anna, and then hopelessness at the prospect of making one. Round and round, his thoughts tumbled like the embers rising from his fire into the night sky.

Chapter 18

April 29, 2012

Salmon River Put-in

They giggled as they wrestled into and zipped up their wetsuits. The thick neoprene would be essential as most of the water running down the Salmon River was pure snowmelt. On one hand, the surging flow would provide an unparalleled adrenaline-laced experience. On the other, just a few minutes in the water could lead to hypothermia. Also called The River of No Return, the Salmon was known for its remoteness as it flowed 425 miles through some of the most rugged terrain in the western United States. This seclusion also made it the ideal spot for these two easily recognizable celebrities to go whitewater rafting in complete privacy.

By privacy, the compromise was their boat complete with river guides and another one full of armed Royal Guards. They were a cumbersome yet necessary part of this holiday. Winston had discreetly arranged for the small contingent of chaperones. They had done a splendid job of remaining just out of eyesight while coordinating with local officials. It had been their mastery of diplomacy and persuasion that had allowed for the young couple to travel with anonymity. However, their proximity on this particular adventure could not be avoided.

"There are just too many variables," Sergeant Bosworth had explained when Winston had mentioned the idea of them going alone. "We would have absolutely no way of providing sufficient coverage from the shore."

Winston had lived with a lifetime of similar concessions. Seldom had he been able to accept an invitation to a neighborhood birthday party or attend the local carnival. It was the price of princedom. He shrugged and acquiesced to the sergeant by means of a compliment. "Very well, Sergeant. I understand. Top notch, as always. I assume you will remain a considerable distance back." Winston fished a waterproof digital camera from a small bag and handed it to the soldier. "And, perhaps, you could snap a few shots?"

The sergeant looked up helplessly as he accepted the camera and assumed his secondary role as "nanny." He actually didn't mind. His team had been selected not only for their individual proficiencies but also for their fondness of the royal family. They had proven their loyalty through the years by standing vigil in the rain, placing their bodies in harm's way and altering their personal lives for the sake of the crown.

Winston wandered off to reunite with his wife as he fished out another small package from his bag. He tucked it behind his back as he walked up behind her and kissed her on the neck. She startled slightly before turning around with a squeal of delight. Even now, her dazzling smile made his head swoon slightly. He collected himself and spoke to her.

"Grace, one year ago, you made me happiest man on earth. For the past twelve months, you have proven yourself over and over as the greatest wife one could ever ask for." He slid the small, gift-wrapped box in front of himself and brought it up chest high. "Happy anniversary, my love."

She demurred playfully and then began to unwrap the gift. Inside of the spring hinged box was an impressive diamond pendant on a gold chain. He removed the jewelry from its case and began to fasten it around her neck. She quickly put her hand to her neck in protest.

"Winston, it's absolutely beautiful, but I don't want to lose it." He continued to attach its clasp and then lowered it into the neckline of her wetsuit.

"Then don't," he said with feigned seriousness. She wrapped her arms around his neck, pulled him close and kissed him warmly.

A singular thought filled his mind. *Success!*

Chapter 19

April 29, 2012

Salmon River Mountain Range

By Joey's reckoning, he was just over ten miles from the trailhead as the crow flies. The terrain had made land navigation somewhat tricky, but he enjoyed the challenge of it. The boulders, cliffs and frequent water crossings had required some Class 3 scrambling, balance and nerve. Last night's campsite had been spectacularly scenic. Positioned at the end of a craggy ridge, sheer cliffs fell almost fifty feet down to the creek below. Fortunately, he had found a steep path on the backside that was barely climbable thanks to some roots that he used for grip and a few natural stairs in the rocky grade. He fell asleep listening to the static of rapids far below.

Today's agenda consisted of some very important tasks. There was breakfast, breathing the mountain air, letting his mind wander, and possibly napping. Yes, today was completely full. After downing some eggs and bacon, he pulled his sleeping bag out of the tent and laid it on the ground under a small opening in the pine ringed canopy overhead. As he laid down, he watched the occasional cloud pass by.

In the last few days of exploring, he found the nearby creek to have a very peculiar quality. Looking upstream, it appeared to be flowing straight out of an enormous slab of rock. Peering through the trees, the steep valley which cradled it appeared to end abruptly at this imposing cliff face. He had contemplated searching for its source, but the terrain had just been too difficult to negotiate. As he studied his topographical map, he noticed that the Salmon River was just beyond the next ridge, but no tributary was shown. The creek's flow was fairly significant, which puzzled him even more. Although the mountains were full of springs, he'd never seen one with this much volume.

The mystery of the creek, thoughts of Anna and questions about the future swirled in his head just like the eddies of the rapids audible far below. With a full stomach and warming streams of sunlight filtering down through the branches, he succumbed to the lure of sleep.

Chapter 20

April 29, 2012

Salmon River

The river guides had signed their non-disclosure agreements and accepted in advance their handsome gratuity for today's trip. As Winston and Grace settled side by side on the yellow inflatable tube, each held their paddle just over the surface of the water. The guide began his safety briefing.

"Alright, when I give the command 'Forward,' I'll follow it with a number. That means I want you to paddle that many strokes and no more. Let's practice. FORWARD THREE!!!" Each of them sank their paddle into the emerald green water and pulled toward the back of the raft. The guide called out the measured strokes, "ONE-TWO-THREE!"

"Alright, the same applies to reverse. Let's try it. "BACK THREE!!!" Winston and Grace clumsily pushed the paddles toward the front of the boat.

"Very good. Now, sometimes, I will give a command like 'RIGHT TWO!' or 'LEFT THREE!' Let's practice. LEFT THREE!!!"

Winston dug his blade into the water and paddled in cadence with their guide's voice, the raft rotating clockwise.

"Very good! Now. RIGHT THREE!" Grace repeated the exercise, which sent the boat spinning in the other direction.

"Now, one last command I may give is 'all in.' If I yell that, you will drop down into the floor directly in front of your tube and place your paddle, blade up with the shaft between your knees. Let's try it. 'ALL IN!!!'"

Winston and Grace dropped to the floor onto their rear ends and held their paddles stiffly in front of their faces like the guards they watched at ceremonies back in Morwell. It all felt very silly and serious at the same time.

"Very good. Now, most important. If you happen to find yourself no longer in the boat and suddenly in a very wet and cold predicament, do not panic. Your personal flotation device is designed to keep you face up with your head above the water." Grace instinctively rolled her head backward so that it made contact with the large flotation collar. "I want you to remember this expression. Nose up, toes up. It will save your life. Many swimmers will try to put their feet down on the riverbed but do not do this. You will be moving downstream at a rapid pace and many of the underwater boulders are like a bear trap. Your foot will become lodged under one of these rocks and the force of the water will bend you forward. You may be fortunate enough to create an air pocket with your body. Or you may find yourself submerged underwater." His voice was much more serious than it had been. "Nose up, toes up. If you lay on your back and position your feet directly ahead of you at water level, you should not become an entrapped swimmer. Your rear end will absorb any impact with underwater obstacles."

Grace was suddenly apprehensive as she looked over at her husband. Her hazel-green eyes peered out from underneath her helmet with a look of sincere concern. Ever the valiant protector, Winston returned her gaze with a smile and squeezed her leg reassuringly.

"Alright, FORWARD THREE!!!"

Chapter 21

April 29, 2012

Chicago, Illinois

Chester's phone rattled around the workspace as it rang and vibrated with a new call.

"Whatcha' got?" he asked, recognizing the caller as a frequent source of his.

A voice with a strong Kenkly accent replied. "It's dem lovebirds. 'Ey've flown the coop."

He sat there frowning as he tried to decipher the vague information. "What are you talking about?"

"The Royal Newlyweds. It's 'eir first anniversary 'oday and nobody knows where 'ey are. The press is goin' wild round here in Morwell!"

"So? They want some privacy. What's the big deal?"

"Nobo'ey knows where 'ey are - except fa' me."

Silence hung between them. Whoever spoke next would have the weaker hand. Chester was a tough customer so he patiently waited. His informant caved.

"'Ey're rumored to be on your side of 'e pond."

Chester's eyebrows lifted in sincere surprise. Suddenly, this story was in his jurisdiction. Exposed-HD's following overseas was still lagging behind expectations, but a juicy story about Taggart's crème de la crème could quickly change all of that. "I'm listening."

"You know 'e drill, mate. Information like 'is sells for a premium. Could be worth a million hits, if you catch my drift."

Chester rolled his eyes. How could he loathe someone who was so much like himself?

"How much?"

"Five grand, U.S. It"ll save you some on the conversion rate."

"I'll go $2,500...IF the info is good. If it's some wild goose chase, the deal's off."

The other voice paused and then continued. Apparently, he needed the cash pretty badly. "'Ee word I got is 'at 'ey boarded a private jet here at Hedgerow and flew west."

"That's it? They flew west? I could look at a compass and have a 25% chance of guessing that." Chester's voice betrayed his irritation.

"All you have to do is look at the flight tracker website. Surely, you can narrow it down. 'Ey flew out on the 26th."

"Tell you what. I'll look into it on my end and see if there's any substance to it. If I can track 'em down, you get two.”

“Two t’ousand?!? From five grand to two t’ousand? I got other people I can call.”

“Call ‘em.” Chester was calling his bluff. There was a pause on the line. He could visualize his source rubbing his forehead as he contemplated the deal.

“You bloody thief. You know you’re robbin’ me blind right now.”

“Thief. Snitch. We’re all in the industry.”

“Two grand. Let me know if you find ‘em. This could be huge for da both of us.”

Chapter 22

April 29, 2012

Salmon River

Two young faces gazed upward at the incomparable ruggedness and beauty of the Salmon River Mountain Range. It was quintessential western splendor. A deep green buffer of lodgepole pines accompanied both sides of the river as Rocky Mountain Douglas Firs provided a secondary barrier further up the step flanks. Bold groves of Engelmann Spruce fought their way even higher toward the peaks only to yield at the tree line at around 11,500'. Above this, the bitter cold and lingering snow leaves only granite ridges pockmarked by volcanic rock.

The pace of this river voyage had been nice. Like the best whitewater rivers, the Salmon maintained the pool-drop, pool-drop tempo which allows for rest between moments of heart-racing excitement. In this emerald green section between the last rapid and the next,

Winston and Grace enjoyed the warmth of the sun as it absorbed into their black wetsuits. This experience was creating permanent memories and deeper emotional bonds between the young husband and wife. It was all a welcome respite from their marathon days of appearances and obligations back in Morwell. Back in that world, the hurried days left one feeling as if they were passengers on a runaway carousel. Their haggard minds were simply too spent to record memories of any worth.

But this – this was a moment. Separated from their electronic devices, they were truly unleashed to absorb everything around them with full faculty of their eyes, nose, ears and skin.

"Forward three," the guide calmly called out. They'd learned that the volume and inflection of his voice was an accurate reflection of the peril they were facing. In these tranquil sections, their paddling was merely an effort to keep the boat drifting in a downstream orientation. However, as rapids appeared, the intensity of his voice served as motivation to dig their paddles in deeply and pull with all their might.

"Alright. We're about to enter Bardwell's Canyon. Legend has it that Clyde Bardwell was a survivor of the Civil War who travelled west to find his fame and fortune. According to the town folk of the day, he would make a brief appearance in the spring only to buy supplies and return to his secret Xanadu. They suspected that he had found the largest of all known veins of gold ore in the western United States. However, curious prospectors that attempted to follow his trail each returned to town with tales that the 'footprints and mule tracks just vanished into thin air' or 'just disappeared into the side of rock wall.' It was as if Clyde Bardwell could somehow pass through some barrier that separated the dimension of our reality and disappear into a world of his own design."

As he told the tale, the guide's gaze drifted upward toward the towering slopes as his voice trailed off. He blinked his eyes, shook his head and suddenly remembered that he was responsible for the potential future king and queen of Taggart.

He cleared his throat. "Eh, umm. Anyway. The canyon contains a long wave-train with a hard dogleg through a box canyon. There is no shoreline in this section so if you do find yourself detached from the boat, remember the adage. 'Nose up, toes up.' Forward two."

Chapter 23

April 29, 2012

Salmon River Mountain Range

What a nap! Joey thought as he stretched his arms above his head and filled his lungs with fresh, clean air. It had been a while since he'd felt this rested. Still lying on top of his sleeping bag, he thought about looking at his watch to check the time but remembered that he'd intentionally left it in his truck back at the trailhead. No matter. The sun was almost directly overhead, which meant that it was about lunchtime. He wasn't really hungry yet, so he just decided to continue laying down under the alpine afghan of overhead tree branches.

I do need to pee, he thought, *but it can wait a few.*

Chapter 24

April 29, 2012

Salmon River

FORWARD THREE!!!" the guide yelled. Grace wondered if she heard a hint of fear in his voice. Unbeknownst to her, the snowpack had been heavy this past winter due to an unusually moist February and March. What had been rain at lower elevations had fallen as almost twenty feet of snow at higher elevations. This past week of warm weather had really amped up the snowmelt, causing the Salmon and any other rivulets in the area to swell. These conditions made the outfitter reluctant to offer the trip for run-of-the-mill tourists, but how often did a company get an opportunity like this? According to the paperwork they were required to sign, the excursion had to be kept in absolute secrecy until the royal couple had successfully completed their holiday and returned to Morwell. Only then could they capitalize on their ferry of famous passengers.

"FORWARD THREE!!!" he shouted again. Grace had shoved her left foot under the tube ahead and her right under the starboard tube. However, she felt like she was riding on one of those mechanical bulls. The violent rocking of the boat as it plowed through foamy troughs and teetered over towering waves had come close to tossing her out. In her peripheral vision, Winston was resolutely focused on the task at hand. His jaw was set and the tendons in his hands were visible as he furiously handled his paddle. His disproportionate strength was causing the boat to rotate clockwise more and more.

This set of rapids seemed to never end and appeared to be getting worse. The scenery flew past as a blur of trees, boulders and froth. The terrain ahead dropped steeply with horizons of water disappearing into what Grace feared was a swirling abyss far below. She tried to remain calm, seeing that there was no alternative except to keep paddling.

"RIGHT FORWARD!!! RIGHT FORWARD!!!" Grace recognized that this was solely her responsibility. Her face became a mask of dread and panic. She tried to sink her paddle, but the highly aerated water gave no purchase. The boat was now spinning toward a boulder ahead where endless tons of water were piling up on its face.

"RIGHT FORWARD!!!" the guide screamed, his voice cracking. Self-preservation had become her primary thought even as her weakened arms began to feel like cold, heavy lead. As the boat careened helpless toward the monolith, she stuck her paddle out in a vain attempt to deflect the collision.

The raft rode up onto the face of the rock, causing the starboard side to rise almost vertically. The next few moments were hard to comprehend. When a human body is flung through space, the brain struggles to recognize and record in a normal fashion. Usually, any recollection is in the form of flashes and frames instead of a continual stream of input. The first frame was of Winston as he was thrown into the floor between the tubes. The second was of the guide straining with all his might to rudder the boat away from the rock. The third was of the water frothing below like an angry green and white volcano.

Suddenly, everything was strangely quiet and almost a reprieve from the terror that she'd been ejected from. Her face registered the icy cold as her eyes instinctively shut. She felt weightless as she toppled like clothes in a washing machine. The barrel-like gurgle of water filled her ears. The brief amnesty ended with a jarring impact to her head. The helmet took the brunt of the blow, which forced her eyes open. She saw only a sea of green and bubbles as her mind fought to determine which way was up toward the surface. She suddenly thought of breath and how long it had been since she had taken her last. Her chest began to tighten and her lungs began to burn as a new level of panic flooded her system.

The water tugged and flung her mercilessly as she

careened off another underwater rock. She unconsciously put her feet together and extended her legs as her foggy mind tried to obey the engrained edict of "Nose up, toes up." Unfortunately, the surface remained several feet away in an unknown direction.

Suddenly, the sensation changed. There was a suction pulling her toward what she perceived to be further downward. Her panic became horror as the darkness around her intensified. *I'm too young. Winston! My whole life is ahead of me. This isn't supposed to be happening.* The thoughts simultaneously intensified and diminished as her oxygen-starved brain struggled to continue functioning.

Her slender frame oriented itself upside down as the hundreds of cubic feet of water were secretly siphoned off through a shaft which had been excavated one hundred forty-five years before. As unconsciousness took over, her eyes closed, and any recording of her brain ceased. Strangely, it still gave orders to keep her mouth closed to keep her lungs from accepting any substance other than air.

The borehole took her deep into the earth under the stoic ridges of granite far above. Thanks to the rules of physics and hydrogeography, the water had to be going somewhere.

Chapter 25

April 29, 2012

Salmon River Mountain Range

Can't wait any longer. Joey's bladder began to protest against his laziness. He slowly staggered to his feet and leisurely sauntered to the lip of the nearby cliff as he unzipped his fly. The ability to urinate virtually anywhere with no facilities was an unrivaled perk of being a guy. He could have simply gone on the ground but, firstly, he didn't want to taint his evergreen oasis. Secondly, it was fun to pee off of tall places. He recalled from a book about deaths in the Grand Canyon that urinating from the rim was a prominent cause of accidents.

He enjoyed the relief in his lower abdomen as he rezipped his pants and stretched once again. No need to wash his hands out here. Anna wasn't watching.

The views never got old. He took in the nearby peaks and let his eyes gaze right once more at the rock face where the creek seemed to mysteriously appear. *Maybe I will try to check that out before I leave.*

The eye more easily detects movement in the edges of its vision than in its center of focus. Something caught his attention down below. He shifted his gaze downward toward the creek where something red was tumbling down a gentle eddy between the rocks. It was attached to something. He squinted as he peered downward through the branches to the water almost five stories below.

What?!? It was so out of place that his mind took a moment to authenticate the details that his visual sensors were providing. It was a body. The limp form was lifeless with arms outstretched. The head lulled faceup with eyes closed and mouth open. It was a girl.

His heart rate increased twenty percent as his brain ordered the delivery of adrenaline in preparation for whatever this situation may require. The focus of his eyes narrowed as his nervous system put his muscles on high alert.

As the body floated past, he wondered, *Is she dead?* Calculations were firing in his prefrontal cortex and hippocampus. The downstream flow would pull her out of sight in just seconds.

Ten minutes to backtrack down the slope if I run. I'd need to skirt the ridge to reach the shore downstream. The current is too fast. There's no time.

Joey's frontal lobe was shut off momentarily. Reasoning would not be needed for what came next. His body pivoted to the left as his leg muscles fired. The sprint quickly accelerated him along the lip of the cliff as the terminus drew near. At the last moment, he veered right and leapt into open space.

Even as he fell, his mind calculated that he would land just a few feet behind the body. *If she's already dead, the rangers might now find two corpses.* He estimated that the water was less than ten feet deep in the pool that was rapidly rushing upward. The wind in his ears began to howl as the weightless hollow of his stomach registered the absurd height of his fall.

He squeezed his boots together and went in at a slight angle, which caused his body to instantly curve under the water. Gratefully, he didn't strike the bottom and felt no injury other than the sting of the surface on his arms and backside. The cold, however, was stunning. Instantly, his cotton work pants and flannel shirt clung to his body like full-body icepacks. He pulled with his arms and kicked toward the light. His mouth opened and drew in a full breath as he broke the surface.

There she was, less than twenty feet ahead. *Go! Go hard!* His body ignored the alarms now flashing in his mind that reminded him he was now in a very dangerous situation. *You could drown. You could get hypothermia. You could break a leg. There is no cell service. Rescue would never find you.*

The better part of him decided that those voices were stupid, weak and selfish. He dug into the water and swam hard. His target was almost within reach. *Almost there! Go!!!*

Satisfaction and relief flooded his system as he grabbed the neoprene covered arm. He flipped himself around so that his legs were now pointing downstream as he positioned his body behind hers and wrapped his arm around her chest. She wasn't going anywhere now without him.

He felt her chest rise and heard a faint moan escape from her lips. This proof of life filled him with gratitude and hope. He was thankful he had not almost just died trying to retrieve a dead body.

He kicked as best as he could while wearing the heavy hiking boots. With his free arm, he slowly made his way toward the shore. He felt the rocky bottom beneath his feet and began to transition into more of a squat. Alive or not, she was still dead weight. Thankfully, he was used to bearing a load and she was visibly slender. With little effort, he dragged her ashore with his arms wrapped underneath hers. He gently laid her down on the sand and moved around to perform a cursory examination.

She was breathing but her lips were almost blue. Her face was pale and her eyes remained closed. A large purplish lump was rising on her forehead. He carefully removed her helmet so that her head could lay flat. He guided his hands over her arms and legs but did not feel any protrusions or deviations in her skeletal system. With the exception of some light abrasions on her face and hands, she looked fairly intact.

Only then did he notice her appearance. A memory from his childhood began to stir. It was from some book or cartoon. *Cinderella? No, that wasn't right. Snow White? Sleeping Beauty?* He couldn't quite place it, but the figure lying in front of him strongly reminded him of a princess. He could not ignore the familiar loveliness of this stranger. For an instant, he thought about looking for a wallet but realized it was foolish.

His brain now began to formulate immediate and short-term plans. His body shivered suddenly as the adrenaline began to wear off. He knew he was in danger and that she was not out of the woods yet, neither literally nor figuratively. He'd heard that you were not supposed to move a victim because of potential spinal cord damage. However, the threat of exposure seemed more pressing. He quickly made a decision and hoisted the limp body over his shoulder.

Chapter 26

April 29, 2012

Salmon River

The two yellow rafts were beached beside one another just downstream from Bardwell's Canyon. Winston stumbled upstream over boulders as he coarsely yelled out. "GRACE! GRACE!!!" Frequently, he ran his fingers through the sides of his hair as his face reflected the nightmarish tragedy that was unfolding.

Upon seeing the duchess fall out, the second boat of royal guards reacted immediately and selflessly. Although the four soldiers and guide were struggling to negotiate the rapids themselves, their divided attention was constantly locked on the yellow raft ahead. There was no leisure or recreation taking place for them. When the other raft had faltered and the body was thrown into the water, Sergeant Bosworth rapidly began to call out orders.

"ROBINSON! BAILEY! IN THE WATER! NOW!" The two young soldiers dropped their paddles and rolled overboard without any hesitation. They looked like dead men as they bobbed face down in the turbulent flow, desperately looking for any sign of Grace.

"GUIDE! DOWNSTREAM, NOW!" The two waterborne men struggled through the raging current toward the other boat. The rear boat shot past them and the boulder as they began to search for any sign of the duchess. The sergeant attempted to stand to get a better vantage point as the boat floundered and flopped through the foaming rapids. His head swiveled in all directions as his unblinking eyes scanned the waters. The other soldier and the guide did their best to keep the boat from capsizing.

As both boats entered the next calm pool, everyone made their way toward a nearby beach and leapt from the boats. The two swimming soldiers quickly made their way ashore. Sergeant Bosworth continued to shout out orders. "Guide! Allen! Take a rescue rope and run downstream. She may have slipped past us. Robinson, Bailey, come with me." The three fought their way up the rocky shore to the last place they had seen her. Hastily yet methodically, they searched in vain for a young lady that Taggart could not afford to lose.

Chapter 27

April 29, 2012

Salmon River Mountain Range

Not even the years of hauling horse feed and bags of concrete could prepare Joey for the physical anguish his body was now feeling. His dunk in the cold water had quickly sapped what little strength remained in his legs and core. With numb hands and shaky knees, he and his unconscious passenger had to take the long way back to camp. The previous day, he'd struggled to make the climb, wearing only a well-fitting backpack. Now with wet clothes, numb feet and 119 pounds of dead weight over his shoulder, it felt impossible.

But time mattered. He'd never treated someone with hypothermia and a potential head injury, but he knew that both he and his patient needed warmth, and quickly. His ragged breaths could not supply enough juice for his oxygen-starved legs. They burned and threatened to give out with each tentative step up the steep slope.

Please help me. Please help me. It wasn't an intentional prayer. That had never really been his thing. The words just naturally seemed to form in his mind. He had already endured so much to reach this point and his stubbornness became pure determination. All of his mental fortitude was concentrated on the next step and then the one after that. The eternity of climbing and pain finally ended as the now familiar plateau greeted him.

They both ended up slumping onto the sleeping bag in a heap. It was the best he could do. *Need to build a fire.* Despite the recent physical excursion, he was shaking almost uncontrollably now. The numbness made his clumsy hands feel like he was wearing frozen boxing gloves as he sifted through the backpack to find the matches. It was a two-handed effort, but he finally slid open the tiny cardboard box. Holding a match between both sets of fingers, he awkwardly tried to rub the flint tip against the strike pad. "Please, please, please." He could not remember a time he'd been so cold that he couldn't strike a match. Everything he needed to survive and help this young lady was at his fingertips - if only his fingertips would cooperate.

Finally, there was a small burst of flame. He frantically looked left and right for some form of kindling. *There!* He hadn't noticed it earlier, but apparently Anna had packed a small New Testament bible in the accessory pocket of his pack. Neither one of them had ever read one. She probably thought it would provide good luck or some form of protection. In a strange way, it currently was. He gingerly slid the burning match between the slightly opened pages and it began to catch.

He reverently laid it in the ashes where last night's fire had been. Even the little heat it generated felt divine. Furiously, he snatched up leaves and small twigs around the campsite before laying them on the delicate flame with tremendous care. Slowly, the flames grew, as did the source of heat. Knowing she needed this worse than he did, thirty seconds of self-care was all he allowed himself. He wrang his hands directly in the top portion of the flames as the smell of burning hair met his nostrils.

Movements were happening more quickly and dexterity was returning. He grabbed any stick he could find and madly broke off nearby limbs. Nothing flammable was off limits. Now for her. He grabbed the corners of his sleeping bag and pulled it parallel to the flames as close as he dared. *Wetsuit on or wetsuit off?* He decided that dry and warm took priority over modesty at the moment. With no ceremony, he flipped her over face down and pulled the zipper, which opened up the back down to the waist. He felt a small degree of relief when he saw that she was wearing a sports bra. He tugged the synthetic material off her shoulders and then tugged it off of her torso and over her hips. It reminded him of playing tug of war with his dog. The wetsuit was momentarily caught on her neoprene booties, which he unzipped and pulled off as well. Not even a moment was given to assess the scenery as he tucked her into his sleeping bag, adjusted her head and then returned his attention to the fire.

Chapter 28
April 29, 2012
Chicago, Illinois

In the darkened workspace, Chester's face was bathed in an eerie pallid glow. He preferred it this way: lights off, screen dimmed, everything typed. To him, the use of books or notepads or even writing implements was archaic. It would be the equivalent of using a horse and buggy as everyone else sped down the interstate at 90 mph.

He was proficient at his business, amazingly so. What had started in high school as a blog for gossip and rumors had become a very profitable enterprise as time, experience and mistakes had honed his skills. The technical aspects were helpful, but it was his network of informants that made the magic happen. The most fascinating facet of this operation was that the offer of money to these individuals erased all manner of dignity or virtue. They were often so greedy for the paycheck (or digital money transfer in today's vernacular) that information was often embellished or even fabricated. It didn't really matter to him. He compared his work to that of a surface miner. In the primitive days of mining, a prospector would go to great lengths to identify a concentrated source of the purest elements. Then, at even great costs and effort, he would burrow into the earth following the vein until it was exhausted. At that point, he would terminate his pursuit and begin the process elsewhere.

Surface mining, however, was the result of an insatiable demand for precious metals. The consumer market demanded copper, gold, silver, and molybdenum in great quantities. Companies responded and adapted by removing literal mountains, busting up and sifting out the good stuff and then discarding the tailings. Only a miniscule fraction of the total excavation was of any value, but it could be harvested at a much greater volume.

Similarly, Chester was interested in quantity over quality. The "processing center" at which he now sat could sift through mountains of data and extract only the juiciest of nuggets for the public's consumption. As the number of his followers and subscribers grew daily, they digitally declared their affirmation of his methods.

He quickly brought up the flight tracker website and initiated a search for April 26th out of Hedgerow Airport. With over 1,300 flights arriving and departing per day, the screen filled with data. He initiated a few filters and the list shrank by over 90%. He narrowed it even further by looking at the passenger manifest that indicated how many people would be flying. *Royalty never goes anywhere alone,* he thought to himself. There was no chance that Winston and Grace had commandeered two pilots and gaily galivanted off to some obscure destination. No. Their position did not allow for such liberties. There would be aides and escorts, guards and drivers. He then supposed that the guards could accomplish the driving, and possibly the other tasks as well.

Bingo! He found it. G7924, departed at 0815, refueled in Gander, Newfoundland and then continued on to Jackson Hole, Wyoming. This was it. His seasoned gut and instinct told him so. Briefly, he lamented the realization that he probably now owed his snitch two grand. However, the potential yield of breaking into the European market could make that chump change. He knew that the devotees in Taggart stumbled over each other to catch a glimpse of the royal couple or hear some new developing tidbit of their lives. *Pathetic but profitable,* he mused.

He opened a new window on his screen and began a search of his personal database of sources in the west. These were his assets and resources. He made certain that they were inventoried and monitored. Some would be maintained. Others would be discarded. His search query was a long shot, but a single name was displayed in the results tab.

Jackpot! Chester did not consider himself a virtuous man. He did not pray or seek the favor of some fabled higher power. In his mind, that was for hopeful saps who didn't have the personal wherewithal to seize what this world had to offer. However, it seemed like the gods of gossip were smiling on him today.

Tony Ferrari used to own and run a large limo service in Manhattan. As Chester understood the story, Tony provided discreet transportation for the city's unsavory characters and business had been very lucrative. However, rivals of the underworld did not appreciate his broad loyalties and demanded his services exclusively. Tony tried to work both sides secretly, but it ended up biting him. To keep from ending up at the bottom of the Hudson River wearing a new pair of concrete shoes, he had to abandon his entire enterprise in the middle of the night and enter his own DIY witness protection program. Now, he operated a small limousine service in Jackson Hole. Apparently, the mafia don't ski very often.

Chapter 29

April 29, 2012

Salmon River

It was the worst abdominal pain he'd ever felt. Worse than the endless sessions of sit-ups from his military training, worse than the time he had food poisoning and worse than hearing that dreadful news on August 31, 1997.

I've lost my wife. She's gone. She's dead. Winston sat on the ground with his elbows on his knees and his head in his hands. There was absolutely no way he could go back to Taggart without her. He could not live with the shame of losing her, of not taking care of her. Leaping into the nearby waters to join her in eternity would have been his strategy except for the faintest possibility that maybe, somehow, she was still alive.

Sergeant Bosworth looked haggard from his efforts but remained vigilant. Steam emanated from the neck of his wetsuit, which had been unzipped just slightly in the back to allow for some ventilation. He took a break from coordinating the search only long enough to console his liege.

"We're not giving up. I've sent the second boat downstream to contact the local authorities. We'll continue the search here until reinforcements arrive. Stay strong, Winston. We mustn't give up hope."

A small radio on his waist crackled with a staticky voice.

"Sergeant! We've made contact with the local patrol. They've offered the use of their helicopter, weather permitting."

Sergeant Bosworth's head whipped up as he realized that he had neglected to monitor the weather. He let an expletive fly as he observed billows of dark clouds rolling over the nearby peaks. The transmission continued.

"I've described the person at large as an important foreign dignitary, female, thin and in good health."

The last descriptor might have seemed odd to the casual observer, but body types play a significant role in survival situations. Although excess body fat hinders mobility and requires additional logistics for extraction, it also provides insulation against the cold and energy stores for protracted periods of separation.

"Copy. Well done. Pass this frequency on to the pilot and keep me updated."

Chapter 30

April 29, 2012

Lemhi County Airbase, Idaho

The high-pitched whine of the Allison Model 250 turboshaft engine continued to increase both in pitch and volume as the rotors of the Bell 206 Long Ranger helicopter slowly began to spin. Seconds later, a deep roar of the secondary compressor added its accompaniment. The pilot and FLIR operator occupied the two front seats as each observed dials, gauges and a host of switches and levers. Wearing green flight suits and military style aviation helmets, they raised their tinted visors as the daylight waned under darkening skies. This call was seemingly no different than the dozens of other search and rescue requests they responded to each year. The FLIR operator called out the description over their closed-loop communication system.

"White female, 30 years of age, 5'9", 120 pounds, wearing a black wetsuit. Last contact was approximately

1130 hours, presumed to be downstream from Bardwell's Canyon."

The GPS coordinates had already been entered into the flight computer, although both men knew the area intimately by virtue of their daily work. As the RPMs of the main and tail rotors synched, the pilot gave the instrument panel one more cursory examination before reaching down and pulling the collective lever upward. As the pitch of the rotors changed, the 2,200 pound aircraft escaped the chains of gravity and began to drift forward and upward over the sea of conifers.

As the helicopter approached the search area, the FLIR operator began to practice his craft. The Forward-Looking InfraRed system was the equivalent of a telescope mounted underneath the fuselage that could detect heat signatures at great distances. The device could sweep a broad area or zoom in to invade the personal space of an individual. As with all technology, though, it had its limitations. Weather greatly hindered its sensitivity. Obviously, a hot heat source would contrast best in a cold climate. Unfortunately, bodies did not always stay warm in such conditions. Neither man acknowledged the possibility that their search target might be permanently cooling off by the minute.

They initially passed over Bardwell's Canyon at 7,000' above sea level, which was about 2,500' above the forest. This still kept them well below the nearby peaks and rapidly lowering cloud cover. The FLIR operator quickly picked up the heat signatures from four people moving along the northern bank of the river. Each was mobile and had the general outline and dimensions of men. They continued scanning downstream and soon located the take-out where the outlines of multiple people, vehicle hoods and exhaust pipes appeared on the display. None appeared to be an incapacitated female. They swept further downstream, knowing that the drift rate of the swift water was around 3 mph. Nothing. The screen flippantly displayed various shades of dark blue and black as the tepid terrain passed by underneath.

After passing the maximum search radius, the pilot turned back upstream and lowered his altitude to just over 5,000. As he flew, he visually scanned the water and beaches below for anything that stood out. As he did, he lamented the fact that most wetsuits were black. Neon yellow would obviously be a better choice, but no one wanted to look like a giant traffic cone in their vacation pics. He glanced over at his FLIR operator and friend, who studiously peered into his screen as his thumb controlled the camera's joystick.

Suddenly, the aircraft dropped and wobbled as a gust of cold air roared down the canyon. The pilot calmy corrected by giving input to the cyclic stick and straightening their course by use of the anti-torque pedals. The FLIR operator never broke his gaze from the task at hand. Both men were comfortable and conditioned to work in varying conditions. However, there was always a point where the risk exceeded the effort. If they went down, more rescuers would then be needed to search for three bodies instead of just one. The incoming weather system was accelerating that inevitable deadline.

"Whaddaya think?" the FLIR operator asked over his communication system.

The pilot looked up and frowned as he corrected through another wind gust.

"We're gonna have to call it soon."

They continued their pass upstream until they reached Bardwell's Canyon. They checked in via radio with ground units, who had no further updates. The pilot decided to climb as high as he dared, making a broad circle over the immediate area. The FLIR operator saw nothing within the canyon walls except for the aforementioned rescue teams. However, as they banked toward the airbase, he casually noticed three dashes of red and yellow heat signatures over the next ridge near a smaller stream. *I wouldn't want to be camping tonight,* he thought to himself.

Chapter 31

April 29, 2012

Salmon River Mountain Range

His shivering finally subsided now that the fire was burning nicely. Joey changed into dry clothes and was boiling some water that he would soon pour into a dehydrated camping meal. Taking inventory of his resources, he had enough food to support one person for the next twenty-four hours. He had planned to hike out tomorrow anyway. He had wrung out his wet clothes, which were now drying on a nearby line he had strung up between two trees. He had a sleeping bag to keep warm tonight. However, it was currently occupied by a slightly bruised but beautiful young lady. His brow furrowed as he contemplated the strange turn of events. *Who are you?* he silently asked himself. *Who is missing you right now?*

Suddenly, an uninvited thought crept into the corners of his mind. They were alone. She was attractive.

She was barely dressed under the cover of his sleeping bag. Joey shook his head and closed his eyes. He refused to entertain such thoughts. Instead, he thought about his sweet Anna and what behavior he would expect from her rescuer if she was ever in such a predicament.

As the water came to a boil, he opened the foil package and carefully poured it in to mix with the powdery chicken noodle soup. According to the instructions, it should be rehydrated and ready to eat in fifteen minutes. Suddenly, the stranger in his sleeping bag moaned. Her head lulled and she tried to open her eyes. He quickly moved to her side to observe and listen. Her eyes fluttered for a moment as she reached for some invisible thing floating overhead.

"Win....Win...." she croaked

"Win? Win what?" he asked. "What do you need?"

The effort seemed to exhaust her, because her arms dropped and she fell back into sleep. There was something about her voice. The enunciation was odd. Either she had truly experienced some head trauma...or she was foreign.

Chapter 32

April 29, 2012

Lemhi County Airbase

I s there a reason you're being so vague with the details?" asked Sheriff Joe Guthrie.

Sergeant Bosworth's dirty face was completely neutral, reflecting neither obstinance nor arrogance. He calmly replied in his swaggered Taggish accent. "Sheriff, your assistance is deeply appreciated by our country, and I assure you that your department will be compensated completely for the use of your officers and resources. However, this matter requires absolute discretion, for political reasons."

"I was at the take-out when you, uh, inserted a man into the patrol vehicle we loaned you. He had what appeared to be a bag over his head. Surely, you can understand my concern."

"Yes, you saw that correctly. However, it was at his own request and for his protection."

The sheriff paused as he mustered the courage to ask his next question. "Was it Harry Styles?" His face broke into a broad grin. "My daughter just loves him and if there is any way we could get either an autograph or possibly even a meet and greet, well, that would just be amazing."

Sergeant Bosworth frowned. The notion that he had devoted the better part of his life to the protection of a pop celebrity was far from flattering. "It is NOT Harry Styles."

The sheriff's smile melted into disappointment. He regrouped and did his best to maintain the upper hand. "Well, I expect a full debriefing after all of this is over."

After the meeting, the sergeant met up with his three corporals. "Any news?" he asked.

Corporal Robinson stepped forward slightly and spoke, "I was debriefing the pilot and his spotter. They observed nothing along the river and are confident that her..." He looked around to make sure their conversation was private. "...majesty is most likely wedged under a rock underwater, which would preclude a heat signature from being detected."

Sergeant Bosworth nodded grimly at this expected hypothesis. Corporal Robison continued, "However, he made an offhanded comment about seeing two campers and a campfire beyond the south ridge near the canyon. They were observed just as they terminated their search due to worsening weather."

Sergeant Bosworth's attention locked onto this bit of peripheral news. His tactical mind began to fabricate possibilities and contingencies. Even with the slimmest likelihood of the duchess being alive, he was not about to leave even the slightest lead open. Despite the almost certain probability of returning without a living, breathing Grace, it was not in him to give up so soon. Other men would have desired a hot shower, some dry clothes and a warm meal. To a man like him, those were mere luxuries that could be enjoyed later. Success in his duties superseded all other desires. He quickly formulated a plan and gave curt orders.

"Robinson. Bailey. Determine the coordinates of that camp and locate any and all access points to that area. Allen. Commandeer as many local officers as you can and establish a perimeter. No one, NO ONE, leaves these woods without inspection."

The three younger soldiers snapped to attention only for the briefest of moments before scattering in hasty obedience.

Chapter 33

April 29, 2012

Salmon River Mountain Range

The campfire and sleeping bag had been effective in warming up the sleeping stranger's skin. When her fingernail was pressed near the cuticle, the reddish color returned almost instantly. Her cheeks displayed the faintest of color and her lips had assumed a rose-like tint. Once again, he wondered at her familiarity.

Now that the external had been warmed, it was time to heat up the inside. He carefully sat down on the sleeping bag and gently lifted her upper body so that she was leaning against his chest. Once she was safely propped up, he took the foil bag of soup and slowly retrieved a spoonful.

"Open up. Come on, now," he said encouragingly. Even though her eyes remained closed, she lazily opened her mouth and allowed him to pour in a small amount. She slowly smacked her lips as she swallowed the reviving sustenance. He laughed a little as she opened her mouth again to signal that she wanted another bite. Spoonful by spoonful, she ate most of the bag. Admittedly, he was hungry. The selfish side of him knew that her fullness meant his emptiness. Her rescue and transport today had really wiped him out. The tightness of his leg and back muscles were constant reminders that he needed energy. The task of getting her out of here tomorrow was too daunting to think about right now.

The scene would have been upsetting to Anna or Winston, seeing the two of them cradled together as he tenderly cared for her. But in the scope of human kindness, it would have made the cover of Time magazine.

As the temperature dropped and the light of day began to wane under darkening skies, his attention was drawn upward just over the next ridge. In the distance, he heard the faint but unmistakable thumping of rotor blades and the red and green flashing lights of a helicopter. Joey thought, *I really wish they knew we were here.*

Chapter 34

April 30, 2012

Salmon River Mountain Range

Sleep deprivation is completely miserable. Add in poor weather conditions, hunger, soreness and stress and it becomes downright agonizing. As the morning sun shyly began to peek over the distant mountaintops, Corporals Allen and Bailey welcomed the warmth of its rays. With their new orders, they had worked with the locals to set up checkpoints at each of the nearby trailheads. Although six had been identified, they had been assigned to the Timber Ridge Recreational Area. Each location had the typical vault toilets, small parking lot and signs indicating the trail mileage to various destinations. The tag numbers of each parked vehicle had been checked through NCIC (National Crime Information Center) as well as the corresponding owner's information. So far, no significant leads had materialized.

Both soldiers had donned their field uniforms, which

had no visible unit patches but included olive green berets. Each had slung their Knight's Stoner rifles across their backs and had fastened drop-leg holsters carrying standard issue Glock 17 pistols. Add to this their scowling facial expressions and the intimidation factor was complete.

Whereas the local officers viewed this solely as a rescue, or more like a recovery, the two soldiers viewed this as a threat to their country and to their duchess. The combined circumstances made the corporals particularly defensive and even cranky. The ownership they felt was merely a natural byproduct of their loyalty. They were exhausted from being awake for the last thirty-six hours and frustrated by their sense of helplessness.

A nearby Jeep Wrangler fired up its engine and idled for about 20 seconds before its reverse lights came on. Corporal Bailey's eyes widened with alarm as the vehicle backed out of its spot and then slowly began to move toward the highway. Bailey suddenly yanked his pistol from his holster and ran toward the parking lot exit to intercept. Allen followed suit and instinctively moved around toward the passenger side of the vehicle.

As it neared the highway, Bailey positioned himself just off the front-left corner of the vehicle and raised his pistol toward the windshield.

"SHUT IT OFF! NOW! TOSS YOUR KEYS OUT OF THE WINDOW AND SHOW ME YOUR HANDS! DO IT NOW!!!" Bailey's eyes were scanning over the top of his sights; the grip on his Glock 17 pistol was stable and practiced. Allen mirrored these actions from the front right corner to avoid a deadly crossfire scenario. The engine died and the driver's window rolled down as a set of keys flew through the air, landing on the pavement nearby. Four sets of hands appeared, palms forward, near the windshield and between the front seat occupants. Bailey moved in closer and adjusted his angle to see inside of the passenger compartment. A wide-eyed man in his 30s and an even more terrified lady, presumably his wife, sat frozen in their seats. Two kids probably less than fourteen years of age were visibly shaking in the back seat. Bailey moved the pistol barrel from occupant to occupant as he scanned the interior of the Jeep.

"Hey! Easy fellas. I think we can take it down a notch or two," a male voice sounded from behind Bailey. He cut his eyes to see one of the local deputies approaching with his hands raised about chest level. His shiny brass name tag read "Willis." Bailey's attention was divided between the family and the approaching officer. He lowered his pistol slightly to a "ready position" and turned his body slightly to cover both parties.

"Can I borrow you for just a sec?" the deputy asked Bailey. Bailey smoothly lowered his pistol before nodding at Allen. Allen lowered his pistol to a ready position but remained in place. Sullenly, Bailey turned to listen to the deputy. Thankfully, he had the professional courtesy to speak quietly so as not to embarrass his new foreign friend.

"Hey, bud. These folks are just out spending time with their family. I don't think they really understand the guns and shouting and what not," the deputy explained.

Bailey's blood was pumping. Although highly trained and disciplined, fatigue and frustration had lit his fuse. Thankfully, the deputy recognized what he was going through.

"Listen, bud. I know you're worried about whoever it is that you're looking for, but we're here to help. We're on your side one hundred percent."

Bailey shot back, "If that were true, why haven't you been searching each of these vehicles. She could be beyond the perimeter by now!"

The deputy took a breath and tried again. "Maybe things are different in Taggart, but your everyday American citizen expects some privacy and to not have guns pointed at their face. We can't just frisk everybody and search through their stuff without cause. It was a stretch to run their license plates and owner's info. The only reason the Sheriff allowed that was for exigent circumstances."

Bailey was visibly trying to calm himself down as the deputy calmly continued. "Look. I'll go smooth things over with these folks and hopefully keep them from filing a complaint or calling the news. The Sheriff said we needed to keep this whole thing as hush-hush as possible."

Bailey finally saw that maybe the deputy wasn't being lazy but quite possibly had a more objective attitude toward the situation that he currently did. His heart didn't feel grateful, but he forced the words from his mouth. "Thank you, Deputy Willis."

The deputy turned to walk toward the Jeep when he suddenly stopped and spoke once more to Bailey.

"I know you can't really say, but we heard that you're looking for Harry Styles' girlfriend."

Chapter 35

April 30, 2012

The Lover's Logpile, Idaho

Winston sat on the stone hearth of the fireplace inside of the romantically decorated cabin. Sergeant Bosworth had secured a nearby vacation property that was normally rented out for newlyweds and couples celebrating their anniversary. It was horribly untimely for poor Winston, but it was within the search area and, most importantly, out of the public's eye.

Bosworth explained, "Your highness, I know you would prefer to be out looking for your wife, but we simply cannot afford the associated risk. If you were observed, the media would land like an enormous flock of pigeons. At your request, the Queen was not made privy to our whereabouts and we should stay the course until this is rectified. We will not stop until we find her, but I need you - she needs you to stay here."

Remaining in this gaudy bungalow while his men did what he should be doing was maddening. He also had been without sleep and his emotions were volatile. Gripped by despair and anguish, he simply held the silent cell phone and rocked on the cold rock fireplace bench, praying that it would only ring in the event of good news.

Chapter 36

April 30, 2012

Salmon River Mountain Range

As he unzipped the tent and stood up outside near the remains of last night's campfire, he stretched and took a deep breath of fresh mountain air. The previous evening's gusty winds had really cleaned out the upper atmosphere, leaving an aquamarine blue sky. Finishing the stretch with a groan, he looked back in the tent at the still snoring figure.

"Time to get you out of here," Joey said to himself. He was a man of simple priorities. Understanding that people came first was not just the result of his upbringing, but also a natural conclusion. He quickly looked around the campsite, inventoried what would be useful today and what should be left behind. Quickly, he rebuilt the fire and began to boil more water. He emptied the rest of the contents from his backpack and selected just a few small items to be placed in his pockets: matches, a folding knife, a flashlight and some trail mix. He used a small piece of rope to make a lanyard for his canteen and then repacked everything else back in the pack. Once the water was boiling, he prepared his last two dehydrated meals. For both of their sakes, he ate the bulk of the calories and only shared a little with her. It concerned him that her eyes still remained closed and that she accepted very little food today. He gave her one more cursory look over as he mustered his resolve.

"It's time to go."

Chapter 37

April 30, 2012

Chicago Illinois

The excitement of the day was palpable. He'd been in this business long enough that nothing shocked him anymore. Any increase in the balance of his bank account brought him only the briefest moment of pleasure but it had never been the true source of his motivation. Today's hunt had ignited something inside. He paused for a moment to analyze his motives and they were two-fold. Firstly, he wanted to expose the royal family for the shallow, self-serving debutantes and narcissists they were. Secondly, he wanted the victory of discovering a well-hidden secret.

Tony, the limousine operator, had confirmed his suspicions. With his heavy Brooklyn based accent, he said, "Yeah, I seen 'em. A couple of frogs came in here earlier in 'da week askin' if 'dey could rent some Tahoes." He pronounced the vehicle model as if it were two separate words. It was doubtful that he realized that "frogs" were a derogatory term for the French and not the Taggish. "I normally don't send my limos out unattended so's I really jacked up the price to let 'em know 'dat's not the way I roll." Tony paused for effect. "Dey didn't even flinch! 'Dey paid the full amount and deposit in cash and 'den stuffed some celebrities in the back before 'dey took off."

"What you mean, 'celebrities'?" Chester asked.

"I don't know. Some kind of rock stars or som'tin. 'Dey had 'em all covered in coats and stuff. I never really saw 'em."

Chester clenched his jaw as if their efforts for discretion were an affront to his entrepreneurial efforts.

"Thanks, Tony. I owe you one. Next time I'm out your way, we'll get a steak dinner. My treat."

Tony smiled at his end of the phone. "Say, 'dat sounds nice. Your treat, right?"

"My treat," Chester said as he also grinned and ended the call.

Chapter 38

April 30, 2012

Timber Ridge Recreational Area

Bailey and Allen were dead on their feet. Despite their many sleepless nights of training and actual missions, their bodies and minds were reaching their limits. Even as they stood near the trailhead, their eyes would involuntarily close as their chins dropped to their chests. Instantly, their heads would snap back up as they began to take deep breaths and blink. It was an interminable and tortuous cycle.

The assisting deputy made small talk with the locals and easily deflected any questions about why strange-looking armed guards were standing nearby. In his casual nature, Deputy Willis garnered their sympathy with his rehearsed tale. "We got a missing little girl we're looking for. She got separated from her group and so we're gonna go round her up before her folks get any more worried than they already are."

The smattering of curious hikers and campers all offered their assistance and concern as they wandered off on their way. The cover story was not inaccurate but painted a slightly obscured version of the truth. *So much the better*, Bailey thought every time he heard the deputy's spiel.

Chapter 39

April 30, 2012

Salmon River Mountain Range

With almost no delicacy, he stuffed the semi-conscious women into two sets of his oversized clothes. It was what he imagined it would be like to dress a very reluctant toddler. He used another section of rope as a makeshift belt to keep his pants sinched around her smaller waist. Lightly, he tapped on her cheeks and even lifted her eyelids, but it was no use. He resigned himself to the fact that she was going to be deadweight.

A helpful human can be carried a fair distance by a fit individual. Joey was no stranger to heavy loads or burdensome tasks. However, this was not a sack of potatoes. Besides, he didn't really know if she had any serious head or neck injuries. With no cell service and no other options, he hefted her off the ground and slumped her over his shoulders in a fireman's carry. *Not too bad,* he reflected as he tested the load.

He looked over the campsite one last time as he mentally itemized every item that would be left behind. The tent was folded and stored beside his backpack and sleeping bag. He had covered the pile of camping gear with branches, not because he thought anyone would ever climb up here, but in hopes that it would provide some protection from the elements.

It was now or never. He had officially said goodbye to the safety of his campsite and committed himself to reaching a place of higher security and comfort tonight. There was no plan B. This was it.

Things did not start off well. As he started to negotiate the steep decline leading away from the hidden plateau, the ground gave way underneath his boot. His right leg shot out in front of him and his left leg stretched backward in a very unnatural and painful split. With the extra weight on his shoulders, they both collapsed to the ground and began to slide. To protect his cargo, he swung her body on top of his and wrapped his arms around her. The rocks and roots tore into his sore back as they bounced and skidded down the uneven slope.

They came to rest at the bottom in a cloud of dust and settling gravel. Joey moaned and tried to take a breath. Nervously, he lifted her face and was relieved to see that he had not damaged her. "Well, that's one way to do it," he spoke to his unresponsive passenger. Eyes closed, she remained silent and oblivious. It stung slightly not to hear a "thank you" but he reminded himself that his feelings currently were not important. With great effort, he untangled himself, hoisted her once more and took his second steps toward home.

Chapter 40

April 30, 2012

Chicago Illinois

It was a long shot, but it was also his only contact in Idaho. He had already placed calls to his associates in Wyoming, Montana and Utah.

"Chatam! How 'ya been? It's Chester! From Chicago? You helped me out last year at the 80s Rock Fest. You got me a free room upgrade?"

Chester wasn't typically this upbeat or jovial with his colleagues, but Chatam had never actually done any work for him. He was simply a desk clerk with a memorable nametag. He remembered the polite and helpful Native-American young man from last fall when he'd visited Blackfoot, Idaho. Three of his favorite rock bands were playing at a casino there and he'd identified Chatam as someone who would bend unusually far to help a stranger. Most people would have felt shame at taking advantage of such a relationship but to Chester, it was just business.

"Hello, Chester. How have you been?" The voice had a choppy formality and a questioning tone. Each syllable was enunciated and almost monotone.

"Man. I've been doing great. I really enjoyed seeing your part of the country. It is beautiful out there!" It was a complete lie. The scenery of Blackfoot is very forgettable when compared to the scenic wonders that surround it. "Say, I actually need some help. Is anything going on at the casino this week? Any big shows or celebrities in town?"

There was a pause before Chatam answered. "Do you like puppets? George and Gandy the Giraffe are headlining tonight. I've heard it's really good."

Chester rolled his eyes and reminded himself to remain polite. "Sorry, Chatam. Sounds great but I'm stuck in Chicago. I've actually been following some news about something big going on out there. Have you seen any black Tahoes driving around together? Probably looks like the secret service or something?"

Another pause. "It's funny that you mention that. My cousin up in Elk Bend said that he saw two yesterday morning and then the same two speeding around this morning."

"Elk Bend? What is that? Some type of zoo or something?"

"No. It is a small town about three hours northwest of here. It's near Salmon."

Chapter 41

April 30, 2012

Salmon, Idaho

*U**ncertain yet centered.* These were the two adjectives that Anna has decided best described her current state of mind. Being alone in the house and in her life the last few days had given her time to reflect. It had been quiet. Not that Joey ever had the gift of gab. However, a house feels different when there's no other life force within its walls. You just know. You feel it. Aloneness has an effect that can be either cathartic or disparaging.

She decided that the time with herself had been helpful. She caught up on some tasks that had been hanging over her head, organized the drawers and closets and indulged herself with a hot fudge Sunday last night at the Sip-N-Shake. Life felt better – less cluttered and more manageable.

Yet, what of her husband? A fear crept into her

thoughts that he would return and announce that he was done. He would declare that he's joining the rodeo or the Navy or some traveling band of gypsies. Clearly, her mind was running away with her. She shook her head and tried to remember the "new Anna." Whatever he decided, she would remain strong. She would be available and willing if his devotion to her persisted, but she had decided that she would not beg him to stay. She loved him too much. The thought of her being a negative draw on his life was too much to bear.

Knowing he was scheduled to come home today, she took time to shower, shave her legs and put on a touch of makeup. Not too much. She selected a white dress with a yellow flowered print that was suitable for spring. She pulled the sides of her hair up with a yellow ribbon and applied some tinted lip gloss as a finishing touch.

Looking in the mirror, she was satisfied with what she saw. Being a woman, contentment with her self-image was something other than vanity. It was a recognition and celebration of what she was. Although she had often dirtied her hands and worn her share of blue jeans doing manual labor, neither of those complimented her design. No. She was pleasant to the eye, hopefully Joey's. And if their marriage survived, maybe she would be the motivation he needed to discover his purpose and design as well.

Chapter 42

April 30, 2012

Salmon River Mountain Range

One foot in front of the other. Come on, Joey. Keep going. It had become his mantra for the last three hours. In all of his recollection, he never remembered being in so much agony or wanting to give up so badly. With every step, his mind begged to drop the weight, ease the pain and save himself. As the miles passed, the begging became shouting demands. The strangest ideas and thoughts invade and bounce around your thoughts in times like these.

He still wondered who this girl was. *Was she a runaway? Not likely. Old enough to be on her own and wearing a wetsuit. The wetsuit: had she been rafting? If so, how did she cross the mountain? The Salmon was clear on the other side of the ridge. Would she be grateful when she came to? What if she belonged to some wealthy family who posted a huge reward?* He thought about the difference a couple of thousand dollars would make to his and Anna's finances. *That's not what this is about,* he sternly reminded himself. He thought again about his sweet Anna and what he would expect from another man if he was in a similar position.

Sweet Anna. He longed to be with her. It didn't matter how or what it looked like. He just wanted to be beside her, to hold her hand. So many things about her were so familiar and comforting to him: the scent of her skin, her blue eyes that speckled like geodes, her laughter – especially when he was its source. Contemplating the memories somehow took the edge off his discomfort and added strength to his weary legs. *One foot in front of the other. Come on, Joey. Keep going.*

Chapter 43

April 30, 2012

The Lover's Logpile, Idaho

Da DA DA Da! Da DA DA da! Winston literally jumped as the cell phone's ring tone began to play. With fumbling fingers, he accepted the call and offered a desperate breathless, "Yes?!?"

"Winston? Where in the world are you, you silly young man? All of Morwell is prowling the streets for any sight of the anniversary couple."

The Queen! Winston's heart began to pound like a child who'd been sent to the principal's office. Right now, he had to decide. *Do I lie? Do I come clean? Do I just hang up and pray that Bosworth finds Grace...alive?!?* It was a terrible acting performance, but he decided on Option #4.

"Oh, hel... ....just about to call.... .....bad reception... are you?" It was the old "my connection is bad" routine. After omitting words and syllables, he even dared to mimic static. "GEHHGGHHH!! GEHHGHHH!!!"

"Winston? Are you there? Is everything well with you and Gracelyn?"

"GEHHGHHH! ....time. Will call you....GEHHGHH!! .....of love. Cheers!"

With that, he quickly pressed the end button and put a closed fist to his mouth. *What have I done? What am I going to do? Bosworth, please!!!*

Chapter 44

April 30, 2012

Salmon River Mountain Range

Getting close. Keep going. It was almost noon and Joey thought the trail was looking very familiar. The woods always look different when you're going the opposite direction. He would have cell phone service soon, possibly at the trailhead. He was sure he would have to give his name to the authorities and explain his part in all of this. On the other hand, she would be receiving all of the attention from the medics or whoever else arrived to help. It didn't matter. She would be safe and his conscience would be clean. Then home to sweet Anna.

He'd grown used to the agonizing numbness in his legs. You wouldn't expect those adjectives to go together but it was the only way to describe the pain he was feeling. His body was making every possible concession to complete the task he was requiring it to perform. Blisters on his feet had become open skin rubbing against wool. His posture had become something more akin to the Hunchback of Notre Dame as he tried not to let the dangling body slip from his stooped shoulders. Try as he may, no position yielded any comfort.

He thought he saw a clearing in the trees ahead and almost swore that he heard the faint sound of a vehicle passing by on the road. *Could the trailhead be that close?* Even though the thought gave him a shot of hope, at that moment, the girl slipped from her position and was unceremoniously dumped onto the rocky trail. He slowly turned to examine his fallen passenger. He wanted to feel sympathetic towards her, but he was absolutely spent. His tank of motivation and compassion had been exhausted.

Realizing that he might as well finish this up, he mustered whatever miniscule strength that remained and wearily scooped her up from the ground. She now lay like a limp rag doll in his arms. As he stood up, his back screamed in protest after being hunched over for so long. However, the migration of agony from his back to his arms was somehow relieving. *One foot in front of the other. Come on, Joey. Let's finish this.*

Chapter 45

April 30, 2012

Timber Ridge Recreation Area

The Knight's Stoner KS-1 rifle was slung across the soldier's chest. The weapon's bolt was "in battery" with a 5.56x45mm NATO round seated in the chamber, the selector-switch on safe. A simple flick of the thumb and only 2.5 pounds of pressure on the trigger would send the firing pin forward, where it would strike the bullet's primer. In the confines of the chamber, the resulting explosion of gunpowder would send the projectile screaming down the spiral-grooved barrel at over 3,100 feet per second. In less than two seconds, it would be over a mile downrange. Whatever, or whoever, was in its path would be having a very bad day.

"I expected something like from these dodgy blokes," the soldier spat with a rancorous Taggish accent.

His partner's mood was equally sour. "Bloody idiots. This will be the second greatest screwing the yanks have ever given us."

Their scowling faces continued to scan the nearby tree line. It had been a terrible assignment from the start. The preliminary op order called for a "backstage" presence: plain clothes, concealed weapons, zero confrontation. They were acting more in the role of invisible babysitters rather than the elite soldiers they had trained for the better part of their adult lives to be. Only the worst of worse-case scenarios could justify any deviation from their commander's mandate. Twenty-four hours prior, it had happened.

Both men were using bravado to hide their inner turmoil. Fear causes many men to become rattled, but their motivating emotion was more akin to a bear protecting its young. If a person was behind this disappearance, no international law or agreement would protect that vile fiend from the extensive wrath they were capable of.

Suddenly, the radios attached to their chests began to squawk. The transmitted voice was shrill with excitement and equally Taggish.

"NORTH PERIMETER! SUSPECT SIGHTED! ALLEN, BAILEY, DO YOU COPY?!?"

Instinctively, both men snapped their rifles to a firing position and looked just over the sights with eyes wide open. In one more second, both men had acquired the target. Adrenaline, duty and anger signaled their leg muscle to fire as both men began to sprint toward the nearby trees. It would take them less than 15 seconds to cover the 100-yard gap, even with their equipment. In the milliseconds it took their minds to process the threat, they instantly knew that the rifles could not be used. The suspect held a female draped in his arms, possibly her.

Their VO2 max was quickly reached but it didn't matter. Whatever pain or discomfort this involved was inconsequential. A nation's fate rested on their shoulders.

"DROP THE GIRL! DROP HER!!!" they both shouted as they drew near. The suspect seemed dazed and was possibly staggering. Perhaps it was their verbal commands or maybe the suspect's exhaustion, but the body in his arms fell to the ground like a sack of grain. One of the soldiers slung his rifle behind his back as the dove onto the fallen form. It was probably to shield her from the veritable explosion that took place a moment later. The second soldier struck the suspect with everything he had, his shoulder spearing him solidly in the ribs. Any remaining wind was forced from the lungs as bones cracked. His feet left the ground as his body was flung backward from the blow of the human projectile. Thankfully, he was knocked unconscious, which spared him from the pummeling that accompanied his subdual.

Chapter 46

April 30, 2012

The Lover's Logpile, Idaho

Da DA DA Da! Da DA DA da!

The bloody mobile again. It must be the queen. She knows.

Da DA DA DA da! Da DA DA da!

Why answer? Accept your fate, Winston. She's gone. You're ruined.

Da DA DA da! Da DA DA da!

Just answer it. Admit to the world you've let your wife die.

Winston continued to stare at the insistent cell phone. His stomach was a cauldron of dread. Reluctantly, he pressed ACCEPT and placed it against his ear but offered no greeting. Sergeant Bosworth spoke.

"We've got her. She's alive."

The cell phone fell to the wooden planked floor and was followed by a recently fainted Duke of Ulbridge.

Chapter 47

April 30, 2012

Salmon, Idaho

What should have been a hero's welcome had suddenly become a hostage situation. As Joey came to, he heard the sound of an engine and a vehicle in motion. The sensation of movement confirmed that he was being transported somewhere.

An ambulance. Thank God. That was thoughtful. Joey's relief and ease was short lived. When he fully opened his eyes, everything was veiled behind a piece of black fabric. He tried to move his arms but they were painfully pinned behind his back.

Am I handcuffed?

His foggy mind started to clear up. He remembered the shouting and then letting something, wait, someone fall to the ground. There was a girl. Not Anna. An impact. Pain in the abdomen. Tunnel vision leading to darkness. But where was he now? He struggled to move but sharp plastic edges dug into his wrists. He was lying down on what felt like vinyl, or maybe leather.

"Hello?" he offered. Silence. More engine noise. More tires rolling on pavement.

"Is everything OK?" He listened for a response. "Am I in some kind of trouble?"

His mind began to clear up as he processed the possibilities. Immediately, he put the pieces together. *They think I kidnapped her.*

He wondered if he should speak. On television shows, criminals were always being advised of their right to remain silent. He thought about asking for a phone call but what he was currently experiencing did not feel like a typical arrest. Plus, it was so cliché.

"I was only trying to help her. I saved her from drowning."

"SHUT YOUR PIE HOLE!!!" a stern voice shouted. Joey thought it odd that the voice sounded very Taggish.

Chapter 48

April 30, 2012

The Lover's Logpile, Idaho

The reunion between Winston and Grace was cinematic. As the Tahoes pulled into the dirt driveway, he burst through the front door and sprinted toward the approaching vehicles.

"GRACE!!!" he yelled hoarsely. "GRACE!!!"

Winston yanked open the rear door of the first Tahoe before it had completely stopped. She was lying in the back seat with her head toward him. Gingerly, he slid his arms underneath her shoulders and laid his head on her chest so that his neck rested against her face. Her skin was warm and alive. *My Grace is alive! Thank you! Thank you!!!* The thoughts would not suffice, so he shouted his appreciation to anyone within earshot.

"Thank you! Thank you all! You've done it! You've brought her back!" Perhaps he was a little carried away in the moment because he shouted, "I shall have you all knighted!"

The two weary royal guards in the front seat were filthy and far less enthusiastic. Yes, they were tremendously grateful this situation had turned out so well, but their satisfaction primarily came from successfully carrying out their charge.

"We've brought along a medic to examine Grace. She's been sequestered in the other vehicle." Winston was performing a cursory examination of his own making sure that his bride still had a nose, two lips, two arms, two legs, no protruding bones and no visible blood. The amount of relief and gratitude coursing through his veins increased by the moment. Then Winston happened to look up and see the other Tahoe through the tinted rear window. The other two soldiers were removing a hooded man from the back seat. He was filthy and looked completely rotten with his arms cuffed behind his back.

Winston's face turned sour as he backed out of the vehicle and made his way around the rear bumper toward the detainee. Emotions were still running high and all of the pent-up stress and anguish instantly manifested itself in rage. Moving fast, Winston closed the distance and threw a hard punch where he expected the face to be. The hooded head whipped to the right as the body went limp, the two soldiers now holding it up by the arms. Winston stood there panting with fists clinched as he watched the guards drag the limp body into the cabin.

Chapter 49

April 30, 2012

Chicago Illinois

H ello, is this Achak, um, BlackRock?"

"Yes" came the flat reply.

"Hi, Achak. My name is Chester Hannigan, from Chicago. I'm a friend of your cousin, Chatam, down in Blackfoot." He embellished by saying they were friends, but the ends justify the means. "He gave me your number and said that you might be available to help me out. I really need some urgent assistance in your neck of the woods." Chester normally didn't use that phrase to describe places, but he hoped it would somehow make him sound more personable and endearing.

"Are you in trouble? Do you need me to come to you?"

Chester was surprised by his blind willingness. "No, no. I'm in Chicago. But I'm looking for some friends. Last I heard, they were going to visit your area, you know, do some sightseeing, but they just dropped off the face of the earth! I'm kinda worried about 'em. Last time I talked to them, they said that they had rented some Black Chevy Tahoes and were going to do some exploring in Idaho. Your cousin said you might have seen them."

The voice was oddly placid and very monotone, much like Chatam's. "Yes. Possibly. I saw two Tahoes yesterday and today. They could be your friends. Are they in trouble?"

"That's just the thing. I don't know. What I really need is some information. Chatam tells me you know a lot of folks around there and it would be such a huge relief just to know they're OK. But I don't want to embarrass them or bother them if everything is fine. Do you know what I mean?"

Chester paused and finally heard a spartan response. "Yes."

"Anyway, I'd be glad to pay you for your time and reimburse you for gas money. How much do you make an hour?"

"$7.25 per hour. It is minimum wage."

"Oh, wow! I think we can do better than that. If you're willing to help me out, I pay $20 an hour starting right now. Start your watch. I want any information you find about those two Tahoes and whoever is in them. Please be discreet. We don't want to bring any unnecessary attention if everything is fine, you know what I'm saying?"

Another laconic response. "Yes."

"Take my number down and call as often as you like.
Oh, I just had a great idea! Do you have a camera?"

Chapter 50

April 30, 2012

Salmon, Idaho

The sky was turning from pink to gray as the sun disappeared behind the mountains. Anna looked out of the window for the tenth time and tried to suppress the growing knot of fear in her stomach. Crazy thoughts were testing the perimeter of her peace, looking for a weak spot to breach.

Maybe he's injured – or dead. Or worse, maybe he doesn't want to come back.

She forced herself to turn her attention back to the living room where she had set the table with their nice plates and glasses. The floor had been vacuumed; nothing was out of place and a scented candle burned on the countertop. The food that she had prepared waited patiently in the oven.

Chapter 51

April 30, 2012

The Lover's Logpile, Idaho

Sergeant Bosworth had not slept in over thirty-six hours. This was not an unfamiliar condition. His life was one of accepted hardship. Whereas your average man slept in, ate donuts, and neglected exercise, Bosworth would not permit that level of softness. No. A man was judged by his strength. Strength allows for the protection of those you care about. It helps you to do the right thing when the majority insist that you're wrong. It gets you to the shore while so many others accept their fate and sink to the bottom. He detested weakness and this was just another exercise in the endless line of challenges that constituted his existence.

"Before you see the patient, I must ask you to sign a non-disclosure agreement. You will understand why once you enter. Since we are not in my home country, there is little recourse to you violating this agreement. With that in mind, we are offering an incentive to be understanding and agreeable to our request for discretion. The terms of our offer are outlined in the contract."

Ashley, the female paramedic, picked up and began to scan the one-page document. She spoke as she read.

"Yeah, I was a little uncertain about the way you guys, um, requested me. The black SUVs, the guns, the foreign accents were all a little bit peculiar."

"And yet, you came willingly. I'm curious as to why?"

"Well, first of all, Daryl, or you know him as Deputy Willis, vouched for you guys. So, there's that. But mostly because someone needed help. That's why I do what I...."

Ashley's eyes grew wide as she finally saw the portion pertaining to her compensation.

"A thousand dollars a month?!? Just to keep my mouth shut? Who is this person? The Queen of Taggart?"

Bosworth said nothing but simply opened the door to the nearby bedroom. Ashley, still holding the contract in one hand, leaned to get a better view of its occupant, who was lying on the bed. Her eyes grew wide and the piece of paper was held against her mouth to hide her surprise.

"Is that...?"

Bosworth finished her question. "The Duchess of Ulbridge? Yes. May I present to you, her highness, Gracelyn Elizabeth Anderton."

Ashley's eyes bounced between her patient and the guard, trying to make sense of this. A new series of thoughts cascaded in her mind. *I'm not supposed to be here. SHE'S not supposed to be here!*

"Well, this explains the need for secrecy." Ashley contemplated the situation for only a moment longer before placing the sheet of paper on the table and signing her name with determination. She regained her composure, grabbed her bag and made her way past Bosworth.

"Pardon me, sir. I need to examine my patient."

The faintest of grins was visible on Bosworth's lips. However, it faded just as quickly as he redirected his attention to the next bedroom. The hardness returned to his eyes as he walked over and opened the door. Inside of this room were Bailey and Allen, who were standing on each side of a chair where a still hooded man was seated. He had regained his consciousness. Hearing the door open and a new presence enter the room, the detainee attempted to communicate.

"Hello?" Joey's words were muffled through the fabric. "I'm willing to cooperate. I really was just trying to help." He paused, wondering if his words were helping or hurting his situation.

Maybe Bosworth would have been more reasonable if he'd been properly rested. As it was, he was more than irritated with this entire country and its mutinous population. The last twenty-four hours had been nothing but grief and toil. Someone was going to pay.

"You will speak only when spoken to. You will answer our questions with only a yes or a no. Is that understood."

Joey turned his face toward the sound of the voice and nodded.

"What is your name?" Bosworth asked sternly.

Joey was rarely receptive to intimidation. He didn't expect to be shot by these men and he hadn't really appreciated the cheap shots either. He answered.

"Yes."

"Yes, what?"

"No?"

"What are you doing? Answer the bloody question!"

"Yes?"

Bosworth realized the game that he now found himself playing. "Alright, smart guy. Answer with more words than yes or no. Speak like a human and we'll treat you like one."

"My name is Joseph Alexander Woodford. Everyone calls me Joey."

Bailey removed a notepad and began notating the information.

"Are you now or have you ever been associated with the Provisional Irish Republican Army?"

"What?!? Are you insane? I'm a farrier from Salmon, Idaho. I shoe horses for a living! I've never even been out of the United States! Give me a break. You guys think I'm a terrorist? Who's the girl? Is she some sort of Irish spy or something? I swear I don't know her!" Joey was almost rambling in reaction to the insinuation.

The guards exchanged looks as Bailey continued to

scribble notes. Bosworth continued his interrogation. "When did you start tracking our convoy? How many are working with you? How did you intercept our itinerary?"

Bosworth felt hamstrung. He'd interrogated multiple prisoners during his career, but now realized that he'd always relied heavily on kinesics. Most humans could utter false words, but getting their bodies to corroborate was an entirely different matter. Most people open their eyes wide when telling lies. You can usually see their entire pupils. Guilty people stretch, yawn, touch their head, all sorts of unconscious movements that an investigator trained in this discipline would recognize. However, the use of the hood and cuffs precluded all of these indicators.

The Sergeant leaned in closely. "You're lying. I know because you were on the far side of the ridge. It's simply not possible for our principal to have fallen overboard and then to have swum over the top of a ten-thousand foot tall mountain."

Even with the hood, it was obvious that Joey was at a loss and confused. He looked down as he tried to make sense of this. He spoke to himself more than to the soldier. "You're right. Something doesn't add up. I figured she was swimming because of the wetsuit. She was in the river? But how? How did she get in my creek? Where does that creek come from? Is there a cave or something? Did you guys see a cave?"

Bailey's fuse was the shortest. "We're asking the

bloody questions here, wanker!"

Bosworth held up his hand, which instantly quelled the fatigued soldier. He signaled to Bailey and Allen, who followed him out of the room. Quietly, he conferred with his two subordinates.

"Your thoughts?"

Bailey and Allen looked at each other to confirm that they were thinking the same thing. Bailey offered his plan simply with a gesture. He slowly slid two fingers across his throat.

Bosworth sighed. He'd once been a young and impetuous soldier. "Thank you, Bailey, but I'm afraid the cloak and dagger days are in our past. The yanks are actually our allies." Straining to think clearly in his current condition, he rubbed his forehead and conceded, "Besides, there are too many witnesses."

Bailey and Allen exchanged surprised looks with each other that their idea had been slightly considered, even in the hypothetical.

Bosworth made a decision. "Clean him up. We'll continue to debrief him, make empty threats about life in prison if he reveals anything to anyone and do our best to erase our tracks. It's all we can do."

Professionalism wanes when one is weary. Bailey and Allen appeared more disappointed that two ten-year olds who'd received socks for Christmas.

Chapter 52

May 1, 2012

Salmon, Idaho

To say Anna had not slept well the previous evening was an understatement. More accurately, she hadn't slept. Before going to bed, she had taken a few bites of a very melancholy meal. She tried to read a book, but her eyes uselessly scanned over a jumble of words as her mind continuously suggested worst case scenarios. She had decided that if Joey had not returned by lunchtime, she would call the Sheriff's office and report him as missing.

She sat at the table with a plate of untouched breakfast, her catatonic stare directed toward a half-empty glass of orange juice. The emptiness of the house was frazzling to her nerves. Her heart started to pound as she heard a vehicle approaching, which did not have the expected rattles and rumble of their minivan. *They're coming to tell me he's dead.*

She stood on weak knees and slowly walked to the door before opening it. A black Chevy Tahoe that looked out of place with mud slung along its sides and wheel wells was pulling to a stop at the end of her walkway. She looked as a uniformed man exited the driver's seat and opened the back door. He helped a man who was obviously injured by the way he slowly stepped down from the vehicle.

Joey!

Anna ran toward him, unaware that she was still barefoot and clothed only in her robe. He looked up a second before she tackled him with her hug.

"Ughhhhhhhh!" he groaned as she squeezed his midsection. "I – can't – breathe." Instantly, she released him, stepped back and inspected him with her eyes.

"Joey, are you hurt?"

He took as deep of a breath as his ribs would allow. "I'm good. Me and the boys here just had a little...misunderstanding."

Anna's eyes bounced between her husband and the two uniformed soldiers who now stood near her front yard.

"Anna, I'd like for you to meet my new compadres, Corporals Allen and Bailey."

Anna eyed them suspiciously then asked Joey, "Where's the van?"

"It's still at the trailhead. I asked for a ride but these guys said that they have a *very tight shedual*," he scornfully mimicked with a horrible Taggish accent. "'*Posthaste*!'" he added while making a smug facial expression.

Chapter 53

May 1, 2012

Salmon, Idaho

Maybe it was in his blood. Maybe he was motivated by the money. Either way, Achak had gleaned an amazing amount of information about the two Tahoes and their occupants over the last twelve hours. By simply asking around town, he had traced their route to Salmon River Extreme. It was a whitewater rafting outfit that offered group and private trips. The office was closed and a note on the door read "Season begins May 15th" and had the phone number listed below. Achak snapped a few photos of two rafts that were sitting on the ground, glistening with water and missing the dust that was visible on all the other rafts still stacked on the trailers.

Next, he drove down to the next takeout, which was about seven miles downstream. The dirt parking lot was covered in tire tracks and he saw some discarded crime scene tape in one of the trash cans. More photos.

From here, he called another cousin who volunteered occasionally with the local rescue squad. He didn't respond to any calls but said that he heard some traffic on the police scanner yesterday directing the on-duty deputies to call the station for some private information. When Achak asked if that was normal, his cousin said that they usually followed that protocol when someone was dead and they didn't want to give the information over the radio for everyone to hear.

On a hunch, he drove to the ambulance service in Salmon and saw both units parked in their respective bays. It didn't hurt to ask, so he spoke with the medics who were watching television in the rec room portion of the station. To their knowledge, no unusual calls had been received in the last day or so, but one of the medics had not shown up for her shift today. They said her name was Ashley.

Chapter 54

May 1, 2012

Salmon, Idaho

Anna held Joey's arm as she eased onto their well-worn plaid sofa. He sank deeply into the cushions, which had long ago given up their resilience. They simply looked at each other without speaking as the Tahoe could be heard accelerating onto the pavement.

There's so much to say, so much to ask, so much I need to know. But not now, Anna thought. Instead, she knelt on the cushions beside him and gently pulled his head into her chest. She rubbed his back and shoulders with her free hand. His hair smelled of leaves and campfire smoke. Normally, he'd be chided for plopping down on the furniture in such a state of disrepair, but this was not normal.

Her husband being escorted home by two Taggish soldiers: not normal. His ribs cracked and his left eye almost swollen shut: not normal. Instead of making them sign non-disclosure agreements, the royal guards had jabbered on about "International Security" and some "Breach of Secrecy" mumbo jumbo. They spoke in menacing tones, but Joey was indifferent to their scare tactics. He still didn't know who the girl was except that she was Taggish or maybe Irish and that she was a "figure of international importance," as the guards had repeatedly said.

After a while, he wanted to get cleaned up, so she helped him take off his clothes. Pine needles and clumps of dirt fell to the floor but she didn't care. The only thing she did care about at this moment was standing in his boxer shorts in the middle of their little bathroom with outdated linoleum flooring. Forget the bills. Forget the stresses of life. Forget about the future. They were together and that was enough.

Anna was sweet to cook fresh eggs, bacon and toast as Joey tried to be helpful by setting the table. He rarely, if ever, complained about pain, but she noticed him wincing each time he reached up for something or leaned over slightly. Lovingly, she said she appreciated his stubborn devotion but explained that what she needed most from him was for him to heal up. Reluctantly, he sat down at the table and relented to being served by her.

Neither prayed before the meal, but they had a habit of waiting for both to be seated before eating. Before the first bite, he reached over, took her hand and squeezed it as he looked her in the eyes and gave a slight smile.

She went first. "So...did ya' catch any fish?"

Joey laughed and immediately regretted it as he hugged his torso. She didn't have a bubbly, extrovertive personality. He supposed that's why her moments of humor were so effective. He played along.

"Yeah, I caught a whopper. It was all I could do to haul it back to camp."

She liked this. Kidding. Smiling. Talking. It had been years.

"OK. Captain Ahab. Start at the beginning. I'm dying to know how you, Joey Woodford, went camping and came home as an international spy."

"A terrorist, actually. It's gonna sound crazy but I promise I'll tell it just like it happened." He took another bite of eggs before he continued. "When Scott suggested that I get away to clear my head, my first thought was that I don't have time. But when you agreed that it might be good for me, well, for us, I thought I'd probably better give it a shot. Nothing else had been working. Well, walking into those woods was like seeing an old buddy. As soon as the traffic noise died down and my cell phone lost coverage, I just felt things starting to fall away. It's like I'd been carrying all this luggage around and didn't realize it. Knowing I had a few days, I just wandered. I'd sit by the creek for an hour, take a nap or climb some ridge just to take in the view. It makes me wonder why all those folks go to a therapist when time in the woods is free."

Anna interjected, "Maybe they need one because they don't go in the woods."

Joey nodded before continuing. "The day before yesterday, I found this amazing camping spot. It was way out in the middle of nowhere. It had this creek that somehow just started from the side of the mountain. I wanted to go find its source, but the terrain was too lumpy there. But up on one of the cliffs, there was this flat spot like a plateau. I found a little game trail up to the top and that's where I set up camp. I'd like to take you there to see it soon."

They hadn't been hiking together in a very long time but, in this moment, she would have agreed to move to Detroit with him.

"Besides, I need to go back and get my camping gear."

"It's still up there?"

Joey nodded. "Well, yesterday, I just took it easy. This spot had everything I needed – great view, the sound of the water flowing past. Just before lunch, I got up to pee and that's when I saw her."

Anna's eyes widened at the mention of this mysterious woman, but she continued listening.

"I wasn't sure what I was seeing at first because it was about fifty feet down through the trees. But it was some girl floating down the stream like a rag doll."

Anna's bewildered expression conveyed her puzzlement. He continued.

"She was floating by and I knew that if I tried to make my way down the trail and around the ridge that she'd be long gone. So, I jumped."

Her eyes went wide. "You jumped? Joey! You could have been killed. Nobody would have ever found you."

He shrugged. "Sorry. I didn't have much time to think about it. Anyway, I got to her and pulled her to the shore. She was unconscious and turning blue so I got her back to the campsite."

"But how?"

He grinned. "It wasn't easy. Thankfully, she wasn't a big mama (the term he often used to describe overweight women) but it still took everything I had."

"Then what?"

Joey shrugged, "I warmed her up. I stripped off her wetsuit, built a fire and heated us up some soup."

A knot formed in Anna's stomach. She was not prone to suspicion, but "stripping off clothes" and "warming her up" were phrases you never wanted your husband to say.

Reading her thoughts. "Nothing happened, Anna. She had on athletic clothes underneath and I put her straight into my sleeping bag. Besides, she was knocked out cold." Showing a touch of defensiveness, he added, "You're not really thinking that I would do something like that?"

"No. I don't. It's just that...when you left, things between us were so uncertain. I just haven't been in a good place when it comes to us."

Joey nodded. "I understand. Me too. But the whole time I was taking care of her, I could only think about you. I thought about what I would want a man to do if he found you out in the middle of nowhere, unconscious. I promise, all I did was take care of her." He paused. "But we did share the tent. We had to."

Anna did her best to ward off the sordid images and scenarios that were testing the fence line of her thoughts.

"Anyway, yesterday I woke up and made us some breakfast before I broke camp. I had to leave everything behind because she was still in no condition to walk." Joey laughed a little. "I feel awful. As soon as I hoisted her up and took my first steps, I slipped and we slid all the way down the mountain. I'm amazed I didn't break her neck!"

Anna acknowledged the action of his story with an amused look.

"The rest of the day was just a long trudge. It was the longest hike of my life. It was probably only six or seven miles but it felt like forty. And just when I think I'm home free, I get tackled by the Taggish twins."

"They tackled you?"

"And kidnapped me. After roughing me up a bit, they put a bag over my head and hauled me off to a cabin. That's where they accused me of being some kind of Irish terrorist."

Anna frowned at the outlandish story. "Joey, this sounds made up. I'm trying hard to believe everything you're telling me, but you do realize how crazy this all sounds, right?"

Joey shrugged. "You met my Taggish buddies. You see my face."

"Alright, gone on," she said as she nodded.

"They kept talking about the girl, saying that they'd been assigned to protect her and that it was impossible for me to have found her where I did. After a while, they all decided to let me go before they got out of town."

"Do you think they were legitimate?"

"Who knows? They weren't American and they didn't kill me. That's about all I know."

"Do you think we should report it? Call the police?"

"They said it wouldn't do any good. They said that they were very good at remaining invisible and covering their tracks."

"Apparently not! They lost the one person they were trying to protect." Anna's mama bear instincts ignited. "And not even a thank you! If you hadn't been there and done what you did, they'd be searching those woods from now until eternity." She was angry and her face showed it. "If I had known – they would have – they better just..." It was one of those moments when the right words would only materialize hours later.

"They said that if I told anyone, there could be 'future repercussions.' I'm not sure what that means but I'm fine with just letting it go."

"Well, I'm not." Anna's arms were crossed and her

eyes were set as she stared across their little living room.

"I don't know, Anna. Things just feel different now. I feel different. I can't really explain it, but I just feel like all of this is going to work out."

She turned and felt his forehead to see if he was warm and then put her hands on both sides of his head as she closely examined his eyes.

"Are you feelin' OK? You didn't feel this way when you left. You had the weight of the world on your shoulders. The only thing that's different is that you've got a black eye and some cracked ribs. How is this better?"

Joey looked off distantly as he answered. "I don't know. I just believe it is...or that it's going to be better. Somehow."

Chapter 55

May 1, 2012

Chicago, Illinois

The images had been electronically transferred after Chester ended his phone call with Achak. He'd had to explain step-by-step how to download the photos from the camera to the computer and then how to attach them to an email. In his metropolitan mind, he imagined his contact living in a teepee with an internet cable running out of it. Anyone from a rural setting was thought of in an inferior or subordinate manner. They were pawns to be used and manipulated. They were assets who he cajoled, flattered and paid in the same way that you added fuel and oil to your car. They were necessary actions required to accomplish a desired result.

As he looked at a digital transcription of their phone call and conversation, he felt an excitement. The trail had gone cold, but the intelligence gathered was enough. He thought of the highly manipulated and obviously fake photos that some of the tabloids used and yet people still bought them. The photos that he'd just downloaded were clear and detailed. They corroborated a theory and could be considered circumstantial evidence. Besides, full revelations were deflating. He could introduce this possibility about the royal couple and correlate it to their mysterious absence in Morwell. The public would make their own assumptions. He was just feeding the rumor mill.

He began to type his first draft.

Awful Anniversary: Royal Retreat to Idaho turns Deadly. Can She Forgive Him?

He knew he was grasping at straws but there was always the possibility of "If." He knew other news sources would be submitting their ideas about where the royal couple had been the last few days. He knew that he was in direct competition and needed to be more convincing with his story. And "If" his story turned out to be true, Exposed-HD would be considered more credible than the less reputable outlets.

He typed an alternate version to weigh against his first.

Royal Nightmare! The Future Crown of Taggart Almost Drowns in Idaho River. Will the Duchess become a Widow?

Chapter 56

May 2, 2012

Hedgerow Airport, Morwell

At 10:12 AM, the tires of a private jet known only as flight G7924 barked on the concrete runway, giving off a faint puff of smoke as they instantly spun up to rolling speed. As the sleek twin engine aircraft rolled to a stop in the private terminal area, an ambulance and three Range Rover SUVs were parked nearby. The whine of the blades was still descending as the door unfolded. Uniformed medics rushed up the stairs and emerged minutes later with a slender figure attached to a backboard. A casual observer would have thought it was a corpse because it was draped in a white sheet.

The body, or patient in this case, was loaded into the awaiting ambulance, which left slowly through the automatic gate. No lights or sirens were used, but it was casually followed by one of the Range Rovers.

The other passengers departed from the plane, one

of which was wearing sunglasses and a hunter's cap with large ear flaps folded down. They quickly entered the two remaining Range Rovers, which also slipped out into the city and blended in with the sea of commuters, trucks and taxis.

Chapter 57

May 2, 2012

Morwell, Taggart

Bancroft leaned over and expertly filled the teacup, which sat on its matching saucer. The set looked regal and expensive and completely at home in the lavish interior of Humbingdon Palace.

The queen spoke without looking at the steaming beverage. "Thank you, Bancroft. Have they returned?"

"Yes, your highness," was all he offered.

Looking very stately, she asked, "Are they well?"

"I...assume so." The moment of pause betrayed him.

"Bancroft. You're faltering. Is there something I should know?"

He quickly gathered himself. "I was told that there was a bit of excitement on their outing. Not much worth noting, I'm sure."

The queen's frown conveyed her disapproval. "Tell Winston I shall like to see him. Today." With this final declaration, she lifted the cup and primly took a sip.

"Yes, your Highness. He shall be here," Bancroft spoke as he turned on his heels and crisply walked toward the oversized, ornate double doors. *Please don't be visibly injured, Winston,* he thought to himself.

Chapter 58
May 2, 2012
Morwell, Taggart

The Royal Guard was tasked not only with the physical protection of the royal family but also their intellectual integrity. There was an image to maintain, and an entire unit was assigned to the task of electronically rooting out any hearsay that could be viewed as derogatory or distasteful. Powerful search engines scoured the web for any reference to a variety of pre-programmed names and keywords. State of the art facial recognition software continually combed through endless photos to make sure each person on the list was displayed in an acceptable manner. Former hackers had been recruited and rehabilitated to aid in the cause. With fiendish pleasure, they would identify the source of a sordid news story and secretly introduce a fatal virus into their servers. They intentionally produced misleading stories and far-fetched lies just to muddy the waters and reduce the credibility of the media in general. With exceptional funding and a digital "license to kill," the covert team of internet assassins dutifully worked in the dim basement room of a nondescript government building downtown.

Olivia "Bloodhound" Ball sat in her padded roller chair with her attention fixed on the three screens mounted above her workstation. Her fingers flew over the keyboard as various windows appeared and shuffled on the three displays. Her eyes were scanning a headline that had just been pinged by their filtering software.

Royal Nightmare! The Future Crown of Taggart Almost Drowns in Idaho River. Will the Duchess become a Widow?

It was from a U.S. website called Exposed-HD. A quick scan revealed that it was VPN protected and originated in Chicago. A few more keys were pressed and a dossier on a Chester Wade Hannigan appeared on the screen. She quickly perused his home address, list of frequent acquaintances, credit score and criminal history. He himself was unimpressive, but his website had grown substantially over the last twelve months. His subscribers were in the tens of thousands and his views were well in the millions. He had little presence in Taggart but apparently was trying to get his foot into the door. She pressed play on the video link. As it began, her headphones began to play loud heavy metal music, which was soon accompanied by a coarse, overly masculine voice.

One year ago, the world watched as Taggart's sweethearts walked the aisle and said 'I do.' They wanted to sneak away for a romantic anniversary trip, but we found them. When you're Royalty, you can run but you can't hide. Our investigators tracked a private flight from Hedgerow Airport to our very own U.S. of A. And where did they wind up? Idaho!

An animation showed a cartoon plane flying westward over the Atlantic Ocean until it arrived at a gold star about 2/3 across the North American continent.

Apparently, the prince has a thing for potatoes. Everything was going swimmingly until one of the lovebirds actually went for a swim. Before our investigators could get an interview, they were whisked away.

The screen showed the whitewater outfitter's sign and then the two boats. The next images were of a beach area and parking lot. Another image zoomed in on a trash can where yellow crime scene tape was hanging loosely from the lid.

First responders in the area are being very hush-hush about the activity that occurred on May 1st but a local paramedic is mysteriously missing and believed to be in the company of the Ulbridge couple.

More images of the ambulance station and then the Jackson Hole airport.

Apparently, the wild west was a little too much for

our foreign friends. Our maybe they're still upset about all that tea we dumped into the harbor. Either way, they got the heck out of dodge.

The previous animation now showed the aircraft returning to Taggart but with caricature figures of Winston and Grace sticking out of the top with their bodies and arms waving wildly in the air.

ANOTHER SECRET EXPOSED, EXPOSED, exposed, exposed. Tons of reverb now made the voice sound like it was in a stadium. *HD STYLE, STYLE, style, style.*

Olivia flagged it and issued an alarm. Within sixty seconds, the digital response appeared on her screen.

THREAT PERCEIVED – DELETE FEED, NEUTRALIZE SOURCE.

Oliva smiled and then opened a new screen. It was a software program that she and her co-workers had developed. A skull and crossbones were on each side of the window. A few taps of the keys and a malicious hoard of ones and zeros were released from their cage as they began honing in on their target at the speed of light.

Target: Chicago.

Chapter 59

May 2, 2012

Morwell, Taggart

Winston's bloodshot eyes remained locked on the sleeping face of his wife, who remained sedated in the hospital bed. A nearby heart monitor beeped healthily and offered some reassurance to his guilty conscience. He berated himself endlessly for his recklessness. He was trying to be spontaneous and romantic, but apparently those virtues were off limits for their kind. He almost dreaded the moment Grace woke up because their future suddenly seemed more like a prison sentence than a honeymoon.

Her eyes suddenly began to flicker, and she absentmindedly reached for the IV taped to her opposite wrist. Winston gently restrained her hand, held it and stood to be in her line of sight. He smiled and tenderly kissed her on the forehead.

"Hello, my love. Welcome back!" he smiled with

sincere delight at seeing her regaining consciousness. "Grace? Do you know me?"

She blinked several more times and looked around the room in a bewildered manner. Returning her attention to him, she said, "Win. What happened? Where are we?"

"We are safe, my love. We are together and that is the important thing."

Grace slowly took in her surroundings and then lifted her arm as she examined the IV. "Was...there an accident?"

This concerned Winston. He had been told by the medical staff that being submerged underwater can cause brain damage. There would be cognitive tests administered once her overall health had been stabilized. They explained that the body takes drastic measures to remain alive in harrowing situations, which can be incredibly taxing. Apparently, it reallocates all non-essential functions toward the basics, like keeping the heart beating. It could take a while before her other systems relaxed and resumed their normal operation.

"Yes, Grace. We were rafting. Whitewater rafting during our trip to the States. You were thrown from the raft and you..." Winston's throat constricted as the memories of that dreadful moment resurfaced.

"I what? Did I drown? Was I revived? Winston, what happened?!?"

He looked up at the ceiling as he searched for the

words. "We...don't really know. You were missing and..." he thought about the mysterious stranger, which still elicited anger in his inner being. The medical staff had thoroughly examined Grace and declared confidently that any injuries she sustained were caused by the river or related collisions. Still, he needed someone to blame other than himself or mother nature.

"And what?" she asked, looking into his eyes for answers.

He composed himself. "There was a man."

Grace's confusion compounded. "A man. What part in this does he play?"

He was relieved that her phrasing was so eloquent. It was a good sign that her brain had not been injured. "When we finally found you, you were in the company of a man. An American." He took the opportunity to highlight their efforts. "But he was taken into custody and questioned at length. He remains a person of interest, but we are fairly confident that his involvement was purely coincidental and that it was not a subversive terrorist plot." He regretted telling her as soon as the words left his mouth. Her reaction was one of pure fear and he realized that he had inadvertently introduced this new possibility into her mind.

He rubbed the outside of her arms and tried to reassure her. "Our men were relentless in their search for you. They honestly left no stone unturned. It was Bosworth who connected the smallest thread of intelligence, which led them to redirect the search to the area where you were found. They pulled off an absolute miracle, Grace!"

Winston was sincerely grateful that this moment was taking place. Anything was better than the alternative. He'd thought about the unbearable shame he would have had to face if he'd returned with a dead wife, or no wife at all. The funeral with no casket. The endless speculation and accusations of the press. He decided they could discuss this more later on.

"My dear, I think you need your rest. We will have the rest of our lives together to make new memories and put this dark chapter well behind us."

Chapter 60
May 3, 2012
Salmon, Idaho

The Ford F-250 turned off the highway onto the dirt driveway at the Traveler's Ranch sign. On the truck's door was a magnetic sign that read "Salmon River Animal Care, Dr. Scott Olens". The day had not started off well for Scott. He just woke up feeling off. He couldn't quite place it, but there was a heavy presence that seemed to be all around him and even in his headspace. He tried to pray but it felt like a bad connection. It felt like static. He tried to read his bible, but his eyes just kept uselessly scanning the same lines of scripture without actually reading them. He'd been on this journey long enough to know that some days were like this. Instead of panicking or complaining, he chose to surrender.

"OK. Lord. I'm gonna keep going. You're in charge even now, and I trust You."

Truth be told, he wasn't feeling very benevolent as he drove toward the ranch to check on the horse he had treated last month. He wasn't feeling charitable or compassionate. He wasn't in the mood for conversations with the ranch owner. If it wasn't so damaging to his reputation, he would have just blown off his appointments and done something mindless, like watch TV.

His forehead wrinkled as he pulled near the barn. It surprised him to see Joey's minivan. Well, Joey's in-law's minivan. Instantly, he was filled with mixed emotions. The last time he'd seen his friend, Joey was in a bad way. Instead of being his usual stoic and resilient self, he was fractured and delicate. It was always awkward to see someone you consider strong when they are in a vulnerable moment. He tried to gear himself up for another session of encouragement. However, his heart wasn't really in it.

Sliding open the large wooden door, he saw Joey kneeling down behind a quarter horse, using a metal tool to scrape rocks from a horseshoe. Scott tried to have a pleasant expression and hopefully a neutral tone.

"Morning, Joey. How's it goin'?"

Joey turned at the sound of his friend's voice, let go of the hoof and tried to stand. He grimaced and grunted with the effort as he hugged his torso. But as he straightened himself out, he actually smiled and stuck his hand out.

"Morning, Scott. It's good to see you, man."

They shook. His offered hand was dusty but neither noticed.

"You OK, Joey? Looks like you got thrown from a bull."

Joey laughed a little, which earned him another wince of pain. "At least that would have been believable. No. This happened on the little camping trip you recommended." Although the statement could have been accusatory, Joey's tone and body language communicated that it was just friendly banter between two men who trusted each other.

"No way! What happened?"

Joey grinned. "You're not gonna believe it but here it goes." And Joey gave Scott a short rundown of finding his ideal camping spot, seeing the girl, hauling her out and then his run-in with the guards.

He listened closely without saying a word. When Joey was done, Scott just stared at him with his mouth slightly open as he tried to process what he'd just been told. "And you're serious? I've never heard you make up tales before, but you understand how ludicrous this sounds, right?"

Joey nodded. "Yep. If you came in here telling me that story, I'd think you were on drugs."

Scott's tone became serious. "You're not...are you?"

"I wish. My ribs are killing me! Anything you can do

about that?"

Scott's smile returned. "I think horse tranquilizers might be a little strong for you. We can tape you up. That'll provide a little stability while they're healing."

Joey lifted his shirt while his friend wrapped thick medical tape around and around his ribcage.

"Man, you'd think I'd be down in the dumps about all this, but I don't know. Something is different. I tried explaining it to Anna, but I really don't know what to say or how to say it."

Listening to and helping another had shifted Scott's focus off of his own bad day. Dark clouds in his mind were parting and he found warmth in the fellowship with his buddy.

"OK. Well, try."

Joey collected his thoughts before he began. "When I went out in the woods, it's like I was remembering things I didn't know I'd forgot. It's like the real me was coming back. I didn't even know he'd gone missing. Right up until I saw the girl, everything I'd been worrying about was clearing up. It was just so easy to prioritize everything in my life, you know. I knew what was important and what I wanted to get back to. It was Anna. It was enjoying my life with her. It was being the best husband I could be for her. It was doin' my best in life and letting the cards fall where they may. It was just this...peace. I don't understand it."

A huge relief filled Scott from the inside out. It swept away any self-pity he may have been feeling earlier and replaced it with an enormous load of gratitude. It wasn't the time to share it, but he'd prayed for his friend the entire time that he was gone. He'd even fasted a day just to show God he meant business. Once again, he saw the proof that God was working behind the scenes in His own unorthodox ways. Understanding this, even the confrontation with the guards and the cracked ribs felt like they would eventually have a purpose.

Scott smiled warmly and put a hand on Joey's shoulder. "Quite an adventure, my friend. Glad you made it back in one piece. Hopefully, that girl wasn't on some Most Wanted list. It'd be terrible if you accidentally helped out some bank robber or serial killer."

"I thought about that. She just looked so darn familiar. I wouldn't be surprised if I happened to see her on TV someday."

Chapter 61

May 3, 2012

Chicago Illinois

Livid, frustrated and oddly curious, Chester continued to stare at his dysfunctional computer. It had given him a buzz when he released the Royal Nightmare video yesterday morning. Instantly, the hits in Taggart were skyrocketing. He just knew this was the first step in expanding into the European market. And then, it stopped. The screen just went blank and froze. The keyboard was unresponsive and the only thing that did work was the power button. Frantically, he powered off and on, off and on but it just kept booting up to the same frozen screen. He called his tech support buddies but none of their suggestions worked. He tried accessing his site from his phone but no dice. He even went down the street to the coffee shop that he frequented but he couldn't view his website there either. It was like some internet judge had sentence his website to death and then chopped off its head.

This irritated and fascinated him. Lots of sites post bogus info about celebrities and royalty. Nothing happens to them. They're allowed to just keep posting lies and smut without any recourse. His, however, had been shut down – hard. But by who? Who could he complain to? How could he verify his suspicions? After giving it considerable thought, he scrolled through his phone until he found the contact he was looking for. It had no actual name but merely a handle that the person went by. He texted because he knew his contact would never actually answer a phone call.

Outgoing: I NEED YOUR ASSISTANCE. WEBSITE DISABLED BY UNKNOWN SOURCE. NEED TO GET BACK ON-LINE. WILL PAY $$$.

He was a little surprised when the response appeared seconds later.

Incoming: WELCOME TO THE BEST REVENGE DEALER IN TOWN. PRICES SO LOW, THEY'RE INSANE! ACT NOW AND WE'LL THROW IN THE 20-PIECE SET FOR FREE!!!

Chester had never used this contact and knew from others that he or she was really a last resort, only to be used in the most extreme circumstance. Well, this qualified. He was on the brink of taking his business and his livelihood to the next level and he wasn't about to let some two-bit hacker stop his momentum. Yes, this definitely called for the Spyder. He replied.

Outgoing: YES. PLEASE SIGN ME UP FOR YOUR PREMIUM SERVICE.

Chapter 62

May 3, 2012

Salmon, Idaho

That evening, after work, Joey got cleaned up before dinner. There were still sharp, breathtaking pains with almost every movement, but he didn't mind. He just felt grateful – grateful to be eating dinner soon, grateful for another day of work and especially grateful to be here with Anna.

He walked up behind her as she stirred the contents of a pot on the stovetop. Sliding his arms around her waist, he pressed against her, buried his face in her hair and drew in through his nose. "Mmmm! Someone smells nice," he said with a sly grin.

She turned around looking genuinely surprised, her mouth open and spoon in hand. "Who is this man that has snuck into my house?!? I could get used to this." She turned around in his arms, being careful not to paint him with tonight's meal. He leaned down and kissed her thoughtfully, meaningfully. As they released, she looked at him and examined him. Women have the ability to see things in men. What she now saw was the man she fell in love with over ten years ago. Life had done its best to sidetrack him and delay his return, but he was here now. She hoped that he would stick around.

As they sat down at the table, he took her hand and squeezed it as he made eye contact with her. They could now begin eating. He complimented the meal and thanked her for cooking. The task of preparing the food generally fell to whoever got home first. Today, that happened to be her. She'd left the daycare a little after three, stopped by the Grocers Cooperative for a few things and then changed clothes for the evening. It just felt like a good idea to her. He asked about her day, which she downplayed, saying, "just another day wrangling wild animals."

Joey grinned and added, "I just now realized that we work in the same industry." They laughed and he winced. After she was done, she asked about his day.

"Saw Scott today."

Anna was interested to hear this. Things had been so muted between them and then Scott comes up with this wilderness retreat idea. Now, their circumstances were more uncertain than ever, but life was somehow better. At that moment, her soul offered her the truth that a difficult life with a good attitude is preferable over an easy one with no hope.

"I told him about it: the camping spot, the girl, the whole strapped-to-the-chair bit. At first, I don't think he believed me. But when I was telling him about it, something came over him." Joey looked off distantly as he recalled the moment.

"He said that he was really glad that it happened and then he just smiled."

Anna frowned. "Was he being sarcastic?"

"You know Scott's not like that. I'm not really sure what he meant by that, but I just can't shake the feeling that something else is going on here. I can't really explain it. But it feels...exciting."

Talk like this made Anna a little uneasy, and also a little excited as well. Life had been so dull and monotonous. The tedium had been like a disease that was creeping into their bodies and minds so slowly that you don't even realize it until you're completely infected. Suddenly, it felt like it was raining – clean, pure water rinsing the past away and creating a clean slate for the future. It was a little frightening for her, but she decided to commit to this and see where it led.

Chapter 63

May 4, 2012

Morwell, Taggart

Grace's sleep had been restless. Through closed eyelids, you could see her pupils twitching as her face contorted in fear. Winston had developed a hair trigger for waking up at the slightest moan or whimper from her. He had always been very caring of her but, in light of the recent events, he was downright motherly.

It was almost midnight when she suddenly gasped and bolted upright in bed. Within five seconds, Winston had pulled the light cord on the beside lamp and turned to be there for Grace. She was staring past the foot of the bed and breathing hard. With mouth open and eyes wide, she held a hand to her chest as she got her bearings.

"Grace! It's alright. I'm here. We're safe." He moved close to her side and put his arm around her. He held her and waited for her to speak.

"It was...so dark and cold. I was tumbling and being pulled...downward."

Winston waited patiently for her to continue.

"I was panicked beyond anything I've ever felt and then...it crept over me."

He intensified his embrace ever so slightly. "What was it, Grace?"

She turned to look at him, horror on her face. "Death."

He closed his eyes and began to weep. "Grace, I am so terribly sorry. This is entirely my fault – the trip, the rafting, and now this. It's all my fault!"

In a strange turn of events, she was comforting him. "Now, now, my precious Winston. We were having a splendid time. It had been some of my favorite moments of our marriage."

"But I almost killed you! I can never forgive myself! Nor should you."

They held each other for some time, gently caressing arms and shoulders. She was the first to speak. "Winston, I do not blame you for what happened. I've been thinking and I do not think that it was sheer luck that I survived or that you found me. I'm coming to believe that something else was working on our behalf. If that is true, then the accident was not entirely unforeseen either."

Winston was lost as he tried to decipher her words. "I don't...understand."

"Neither do I. At least, not yet."

Chapter 64

May 5, 2012

Salmon, Idaho

She wasn't sure how he'd found a picnic basket, but she loved the image of him standing there, holding it in one hand and offering the open door of the minivan with the other. The practical side of her did the math in her head.

It's Saturday. We have to eat anyway so you can't count the food. We'll probably burn two dollars in gas. Pretty cheap date!

Money aside, she was thrilled that they were doing something. Joey had a glint in his eye as he refused to tell her where they were going. With the windows down and music playing on the radio, this spring day was competing for the title of "perfect."

They drove only a few minutes north of town and turned left at a sign for Morgan Bar Recreation Site. It was a day use area beside the river that they'd driven past countless times but never stopped to investigate. As they pulled to a stop, he held his hand up as she attempted to open the door. He quickly moved around to the front before opening her door like a chauffeur. She exited dramatically and did her best celebrity impression. "Thank you, James," she said with a deep syrupy voice. "Now, be a dear and collect our things."

He played along by saluting with his palm facing out. "Yes, ma'am!"

It was silly but she loved it. It felt like they were making up for lost time and were being given something that was stolen from them. Joey sat the basket down on the bench of the picnic table and retrieved from it a small bouquet of handpicked wildflowers. Anna's eyes lit up as she took them. Then, he pulled out one of those red and white checkered tablecloths, which he spread across the table. She laughed as he ran from corner to corner, trying to keep the breeze from ripping it away. Finally, he picked up four small stones and set them on each edge.

"That oughta' do," he said as he dusted off his hands and began to retrieve their sandwiches he had made. She loved him so much.

They sat down, clasped hands and squeezed before taking their first bites. They sat across from each other, gazing and smiling. The moment did not necessarily require words. The company of each other was sufficient.

"Do you think you'll ever hear anything from your Taggish *friends* again?" Anna asked, exaggerating the word friends.

"Man, I hope not." Joey answered as he unconsciously touched his left temple where his eye had almost returned to normal.

"Does that seem fair to you? What they did? How they treated you?"

Joey finished chewing his bite as he thought about it. "I don't know. It was a strange situation. Part of me kinda' understood why they were actin' that way. Lord knows I'd be upset if you went missing. No tellin' who would get bopped in the head!" he laughed and winced at the same time. Grimacing was quickly becoming his newest habit. "I've thought about it for hours and I just don't feel wrong for anything I did. What they did or do from here is up to them."

Anna looked at this man she called her husband. It's like some outer shell had cracked and flaked away, revealing this gallant, caring, knight inside. She took his hand across the table and looked him in the eyes.

"I love you, Joey."

Chapter 65

May 5, 2012

Location Unknown

The gorgeous weather outside on this Saturday afternoon was completely irrelevant to the person working in this dark crypt. The glow of computer screens and the whirr of hard-drive cooling fans were the only sensations perceived by the operator, who sat in a high-back black leather chair.

Had Spyder ventured to go outside, squinting eyes might have wondered what the blinding circular source of heat looming overhead was. No. Spyder had access to the entire world and sometimes outer space simply by clicking a mouse, typing some commands or penetrating some almost impenetrable firewall. Although a premium was required to contract with this enigmatic and legendary hacker, results were guaranteed. Seriously, there was a 100% full refund if the goal was not accomplished or if the client was discovered.

Financial gain was the easiest way to measure success, but the real gratification came from being invisible and sovereign. Spyder had yet to meet anyone who posed a threat. Remaining on top of the hill, however, required almost a religious devotion to the craft and a complete lack of respect for authority. Spyder saw titles, governmental entities and borders as man-made, arbitrary constructions. They had all changed drastically over the centuries, which diminished their credibility according to this strange reasoning.

Fingers were interlaced and cracked before this newest job (or challenge) was approached. Sessions of this nature could continue for over twenty-four hours straight. It often became a game of cat and mouse, except that Spyder preferred to think of it as tarantula and cricket. It required patience and chess-like strategy as the opponent was lured into the web, not realizing that they had just signed their own death warrant. The death was always virtual and never physical, but the triumph Spyder felt was akin to what a spy or Viking must have experienced.

The game began as a tracking program was initiated. Security protocols automatically started to scan for external monitoring or tracing activity. The search began from Chicago and immediately made a connection to a terminal in Spain. The track then continued into Germany, France and ended in Taggart. A map was enlarged, which traced the origin to an obscure address in downtown Morwell. Just as quickly as the search had begun, it self-terminated and automatically erased its tracks. The entire process had taken less than five seconds. Any security countermeasures that had been activated were just now registering potential danger and their searches scanned only empty space on the web.

"Too easy," Spyder muttered disappointedly.

Chapter 66

May 6, 2012

Morwell, Taggart

Olivia's supervisor made her rounds past each terminal about an hour after everyone's shift began. Since her crew had a reputation of proficiency and dedication, it was more of a protocol of etiquette rather than an operations update. As she neared the "Bloodhound's" workstation, she noticed that Oliva was perched forward in her chair with her face closer to the screen than normal, her eyes darting back and forth between open windows.

"Good morning, Olivia. How goes it today?"

Engrossed in her work, it took her a moment to realize she was being spoken to. "Oh! I'm sorry. I was just checking on a security alert that popped up last night." She continued to click and operate her mouse as she spoke.

Her supervisor leaned over and observed that at 2:12

AM, a breach was attempted on their firewall. It ended as soon as it began. *Probably a lower-level hacker that was testing their skill level or maybe some bugger who explored just a bit too far,* she thought to herself. "Any trail?"

"Not a trace. I can't even see a VPN or source. It's almost as if the security program suffered a glitch."

The seasoned head of the cybersecurity department frowned. *It's a bit too clean, isn't it?* "Log it. Run a diagnostic on the firewall and review the activity journal for the last forty-eight hours. If someone was curious about us, we probably gave them a reason to be."

Chapter 67

May 6, 2012

Salmon, Idaho

Joey and Anna slept well last night, woke up feeling refreshed around 7:00 AM, and were enjoying the laziness of a beautiful Idaho Sunday. Sunlight flickered through thin curtains, which fluttered in the breeze from the cracked windows. Springtime invited itself inside this time of year.

Anna placed her head on Joey's chest and pondered the last few days. She had never stopped loving Joey. However, the last few days had made that daily intentional decision much easier, even natural. The picnic, conversation during meals, the playfulness – it had been a breath of fresh air for their relationship. She wondered how long it would last and, optimistically, how far it could go.

She tilted her head so that she was face to face with Joey, her chin on his sternum. Admiring his features, she asked, "Where would you want to go if we won a vacation? Anywhere in the world."

Only two weeks ago, this question might have felt like an insinuation meant to cause guilt and frustration. Their current financial state could probably get them to the Utah state line. However, the level of trust was currently high between them, so he thought about it before answering.

"Have you ever seen those islands in the Mediterranean that have all the white houses leading up the hillside?"

"I think that's in Greece. San...ta rini, or something?"

"I guess." Joey gazed off distantly. "Well, that looks about as close to paradise as I can imagine. I think about sitting on that beach, maybe a nice drink, just watchin' the sunset." He returned his attention to her. "As long as you'll come, too."

She must have liked his answer because she laid her head on his chest again and tenderly placed her hand on his injured ribs.

"How about you?" he asked.

Anna thought for several minutes. She'd been to the surrounding states but most of that had been as a kid. *Maybe New York or San Diego? Not unless a miracle happened.* She didn't dare expand her dreams to somewhere across an ocean. A stab of panic and hopelessness suddenly threatened to ruin this perfect moment. Refusing to let that happen, she blurted out,

"FIJI!!!" It was a little more enthusiastic than the mood allowed but she continued. "I wanna stay in one of those bungalows that's built out over the water. I want room service and tropical breezes and snorkeling with tropical fish!"

"Really sensing a strong tropical theme, here."

She tilted her head again, looked at him and pouted. "Idaho really needs a beach."

Joey lightly stroked her back as they digested their fantasies of traveling. The old him would have silently lamented his inability to give these experiences to Anna. But things felt different now. Hopeful even.

"Fiji, huh?" Enigmatically, Joey said, "That's gonna be nice."

Chapter 68
May 6, 2012
Morwell, Taggart

Grace's rest and recovery continued throughout the weekend. Taggart's finest medical professionals had run a battery of tests that declared her physically well despite a few lingering bruises.

However, inner pain is more difficult to diagnose and even harder to treat. She just wasn't feeling quite like herself. There was a heaviness and even a darkness that was hovering over her countenance like a smothering wet blanket. She tried to describe it to the mental health counselor, and even Winston, but it was almost impossible to articulate.

"It feels as if I've misplaced something terribly important and yet I don't know what it is I've misplaced."

Winston listened sympathetically but had no answers.

Grace tried again. "It's like I've forgotten the birthday of a loved one but I don't know who to call or to apologize to. It's maddeningly frustrating." Her familiar smile and light disposition had been missing ever since the accident.

Winston would have surrendered his right to the throne to get it back. Unfortunately, these things take time to sort out. He just hoped that she could.

Chapter 69

May 12, 2012

Salmon, Idaho

Another work week ended and had been much like any other. Joey had been making his rounds and tending to the area's horses. He came home dirty and hungry each night, and she loved him for it. Their truck was still gone, bills were still piling up and buckets had been set out in the living room when it rained last night. But those problems were not a priority.

Anna finished her shift at the daycare and wondered on the way home why she wasn't more worried. Maybe Joey's new attitude was infectious? Maybe it was better to get foreclosed and go bankrupt than to live your life in dread? Could she trust that everything would be OK? Could she discipline herself not to focus on or express any fears to Joey? What good had that really done?

She turned onto the dirt drive and stopped to get the mail from their tilted, rusty mailbox. As she forced the flimsy door back into its closed position, she reflected that everything they owned was tilted and rusty. Lovingly, she traced her fingers around its curved top. She purposefully decided to be thankful they had a mailbox.

Walking into the house, she thought back wistfully to their picnic and appreciated Joey's newfound thoughtfulness. Not to be outdone, she decided to be creative. They had some frozen ducks that had been given to them by a neighbor. There were some potatoes she could bake and they had fresh salad. She dug around in the cabinets until she found their nice placemats and some candlesticks.

After starting dinner and setting the table, she went to her closet to look through her dresses. After selecting one that was date worthy, she began to apply a little more makeup and lip gloss before inserting her fake diamond earrings. After she was done, she examined herself in the mirror and was pleased with what she saw. Hopefully, Joey would be too. Tonight, they would eat like royalty.

Chapter 70

May 12, 2012

Morwell, Taggart

Olivia logged off of her terminal and performed a mental recollection of the tasks she'd completed this week. The system diagnostic had gone swimmingly and no more breaches had been attempted, or at least detected. Their department released some bogus stories about Winston and Grace just to confuse the masses and thwart anyone that might have actual news about their anniversary whereabouts.

She'd never met the royal couple but would enjoy the opportunity. At times, she contemplated the small army that was required to support and facilitate their agendas. There were personal assistants, drivers, cooks, personal trainers, fashion coordinators, guards, cybersecurity personnel (such as herself) and probably a battalion of others she had not thought about.

One could question the justification of such

extravagance and excess, but Olivia did not see it that way. Taggart was a special place, to her personally and in the world. Perhaps, such a place needed fairy tales, princes and princesses. She was glad to be a small part of it all.

Chapter 71

May 12, 2012

Morwell, Taggart

The week had been miserable for Winston. Grace's thrashing and yelling had prevented any meaningful sleep and he was worried about her. She had refused the doctor's offer of a sedative and was becoming more frustrated about not being able to remember this missing piece of information that her subconscious refused to ignore. All the while, he feared that she might never get better and that it would be solely his fault.

That Friday night, they turned in as they normally did. He offered everything he could think of to make her comfortable and assured her that he loved her very much.

"I know, Win," she had replied. He could tell that it wasn't that she didn't love him. She was just so distracted by this enigma.

After a while, his thoughts subsided and

consciousness slipped away. He was getting to that point of sliding down into deeper sleep when something rudely ripped him from his rest.

Grace sat completely upright and gasped loudly. Her eyes were wide with either terror or recollection. In the dim light of the room, he couldn't tell.

"What is it, my love?!? What do you need? Absolutely anything!" he pleaded after sitting up beside her.

She turned and looked him in the eye with the strangest expression. "I know what it is."

Chapter 72

May 13, 2012

Chicago, Illinois

He held a grudge. It wasn't the ruined computer hardware or the cost of hiring Spyder that fueled his ire. It was that someone had sabotaged and stolen his hard work. Sure, he got that most people thought websites like his were sleezy or, at best, deceiving. But it was honest work. He provided a service that a large percentage of the populace enjoyed and was willing to pay for. People worshipped celebrities and were hungry to know the details of their lives, especially when they were juicy. He had found his golden ticket, fair and square. Then, someone came along and swiped it. He couldn't just let that go.

It had taken several thousand dollars, but his new computer had been set up and the website had been recovered. He thought about reposting the video, but news had a very short expiration date. Besides, several other news outlets had posted equally convincing stories about Winston and Grace being in Dubai or China or even Norway.

However, this was now personal. Each piece of equipment that had been purchased and each day that his website was down was a reminder that someone had intentionally nuked his operation. He was convinced that his story had been (mostly) accurate and that's why it was eliminated so effectively. Whoever it did this was not invincible. You could get to anybody as long as you had one thing: patience.

Chapter 73
May 13, 2012
Salmon, Idaho

It was the evening before another week started. Usually, Sundays would be slightly tainted knowing that the weekend was over and that another five days of drudgery were about to begin. However, things had been going so well for them. Not them as individuals, but them as a married couple. In their wedding ceremony, the preacher had used forgettable phrases like "two become one" and "sharing your lives" and it was starting to click for the two of them. They could carry each other's burdens, celebrate small victories with one another and make sure that the other never faced a challenge alone.

They washed the dishes together with Joey manning the sink and Anna using the kitchen towel to dry. It was efficient and even fun.

Putting up the last dish, Joey shut the cabinet door and asked "So whatcha' wanna do?"

They had about two hours before bedtime. Anna was about to answer when there was a knock on the door. She looked toward the source of the sound and then back at Joey.

"Are you expecting anybody?"

"No. Are you?"

Knocks after dark on Sunday nights were odd. A neighbor in need? The police with bad news?

They both went over to their shabby, outdated wood paneled door and pulled it open. Anna immediately recognized the couple standing on their doorstep and gasped. Joey did not.

Chapter 74

May 13, 2012

Unknown Location

It was not so much a hunt but a stalk. Spyder had learned that impatience can spook your prey and expose your location. Methodically, the hacker delicately probed leads and set up traps. These were digital traps but were just as effective as the ones used to ensnare grizzlies. Spdyer set up a hunting blind near the area of interest. In this case, Morwell, Taggart. Government agencies were not a threat to be taken likely. It's not that their technology was necessarily superior to the private sector. It's just that the consequences of getting caught were infinitely more serious.

A window of the computer screen began to indicate activity. Spyder looked at the data and picked up the cell phone. A text:

Incoming: CROWNS AIRBORNE AGAIN. SAME

PATH AS BEFORE.

    Outgoing: OUTSTANDING! ASSETS IN PLACE. I'M HEADED WEST. KEEP ME UPDATED.

Chapter 75
May 13, 2012
Salmon, Idaho

Winston felt embarrassed and awkward standing on the front porch of a shabby little house whose owner he had sucker punched in the face just over a week ago. However, he had promised Grace during her convalescence that he would do anything to help her. When she had woken up with eyes wide, he had no idea what that would actually consist of.

The prior night, as he lay beside Grace, he anguished over her condition. The guilt of knowing that her suffering was the result of his "wanton recklessness in regard to her safety." When she gasped and sat up in bed, he assumed it was just another night terror. However, when she looked at him and said, "I know what it is," he listened with rapt curiosity.

Grace began to ramble as she suddenly recalled the

details. "I remember! We were rafting. In Idaho!" She put her hand to her chest and took a deep breath of relief. She actually smiled for the first time since the incident, which brought great joy to Winston. She blinked a few times, turned back to Winston and took his hand. "My sweet Winston. Our anniversary trip that you worked so hard to prepare for." Her absence of anger and graciousness brought sudden tears to his eyes. He swallowed and tried to compose himself. "We'd been having such a wonderful adventure with the helicopter flight over the Grand Tetons, Old Faithful at Yellowstone and even our trip down the Salmon." He was amazed and grateful that her memory had now returned and that she remembered these things so clearly.

Her face suddenly turned dour. "And then we went through the rapids. I...I've never felt so helpless." Winston strengthened his grip with her hand. "It was black and cold. It felt like what I imagine death to be like. Then, it was as if I was pulled down into a giant drain of sorts. I was being pulled downward, into the earth. At this point, I was grateful that I fell unconscious to spare me from further terror." Winston ached for her and wished that he could have somehow taken her place; for him to bear the awful weight of these dreadful memories instead of her.

Grace blinked and shook her head as she struggled to recall more. "And then...there was a man." Unconsciously, Winston's concerned expression morphed into one of suspicion. "My eyes remained closed. At the time, it would have taken more strength than I possessed to open them and see my savior."

My savior?!? "Grace, please go on. I must hear this," Winston urgently goaded.

She composed her thoughts. "Do you remember a time when you were a child and your father lifted you from your bed as you slept? Even though you were truly out of it, you still felt his embrace and were certain of your security."

Winston thought deeply and recalled the feeling. He was six and had been suffering from a terrible fever. Although they had nannies, he distinctly remembered his father coming into his room, picking him up and holding him securely. His father had mumbled some silly children's song and blew on his forehead to provide some relief. It was one of his fondest memories.

"He carried me. We bounced and stumbled and it seemed to take an eternity," she paused before continuing, "But I remember feeling warmth return to me. He fed me." She looked up and searched the ceiling for some way to understand this. "Oh, Winston. He was my angel! He saved me. Do you know him?"

Winston turned away with a blank expression as he muttered useless syllables. "I, um, he..."

"Winston, please tell me you found him. We are deeply indebted to him."

He looked for a rock to crawl under. He considered

jumping from the window. How could he tell his wife that he'd reacted in the completely opposite way to what was appropriate? He could blame it on the guards, but no. Hadn't he offered to have them knighted? *Oh dear.* His expression must have betrayed his inner turmoil.

"Win. Is this man alive? Has he perished in the rescue?"

He shrugged and opened his mouth, although only strained vowel sounds escaped.

She frowned. "Winston. There is something you're not telling me. Do not hold anything back. You must help me fill in the gaps."

In desperation, he went on the offensive. "Did he...?"

"Did he what?"

"Did he...take advantage of you?"

She looked appalled. "What? No! Winston, this man gave everything for me. His food, his clothing, his comfort. I'm quite certain he carried me for miles upon his back. This man is a selfless hero!"

He abruptly felt sick. There was no way to save face. "I might have...struck him."

Grace's mouth fell open as she stared at her husband in horror.

He began to babble. "It, well, it's just that we thought we had lost you! Everyone was so frantic. We'd been up all night and when we learned that there was the faintest possibility that you might be in the company of another..." He turned grim at the memory. He grimaced and clinched his fists. "I would have killed to have found you. I would have given myself in your place. When I saw him, everything that had been building up over the last day or so just erupted."

Grace was struggling to comprehend this new information. "Was he vile? Did he have the appearance of a villain?"

Stupidly, he answered. "I'm not sure. He had a bag over his head."

"WHAT?!? Winston! This is absolutely absurd!"

Needless to say, Winston made a late-night phone call and one of the family's private jets winged westward within the hour.

Joey made some basic observations. The girl was strikingly beautiful, and it only took a moment to realize that she was the same person he'd pulled from the creek. He also assumed that the well-dressed guy to her left was the boyfriend or husband who had arranged for him to be kidnapped. The side of his skull where he'd been punched recommended swift revenge, but Joey refrained. The girl spoke.

"Hello. My name is Grace and this is my husband, Winston." She extended her hand to Anna, who blankly looked down at it. She didn't know whether to shake it or curtsy. Finally, she composed herself, took Grace's hand and responded with a question.

"Your Highness?"

"Please, goodness no! Grace will be fine." She turned to Joey and looked at him squarely in the face. Winston stood by with a strange blend of uncomfortable stoicism. Although it broke every rule of royal etiquette, she took a step toward him and embraced him with both arms. It was a full bear hug, entirely inappropriate for someone of her station, but necessary nonetheless. Joey was completely caught off guard and awkwardly patted her on the back. After a moment, she released him. Her eyes were moist and the quiver in the voice conveyed her emotion. "Joey. We are so indebted and grateful to you." Her sincerity once again overwhelmed her formality. "You saved my life!"

A brief moment passed as the two couples searched each other's faces. Grace cleared her throat in the direction of Winston, which spurned him to action.

He smiled politely and extended his hand first to Joey. His rehearsed words came out more like a speech. "The royal family would like to express its gratitude for, ooogh!"

Grace's elbow caught him in the ribs and her scowl burned holes into his eyes. He corrected and rightly assumed his role as a grateful husband and decent human being.

"I'm sorry. I was the one that struck you. I ordered our guards to take you into custody and have you interrogated." It felt strange to apologize to a man who was, in truth, both a commoner and a yank. "I was so frightened at the time and I assumed the worst about you. It was completely unacceptable, and I now avail myself to your retribution."

Winston closed his eyes and turned his face so that it was an available and obvious target. He waited for the blow that never came.

"Who are you people?" Joey asked. "I figured that you were a big deal with all the security and helicopters. You're obviously not from around here."

With her typical poise and grace, Grace explained. "We are from Taggart and my husband is part of the royal family. Do you remember Princess Joanna? Lady J?"

The wheels in Joey's mind began to turn as he made the connection. He nodded and spoke to Winston. "Huh. That was your mom. OK. Things are starting to make a little more sense now."

Winston replied, "Yes. It's true. That was the reason we took such drastic measures, and I would be greatly relieved if you would now take your revenge." Once again, he tightly closed his eyes like a prisoner waiting for the firing squad.

"Would you stop it." Grace insisted. "He's not going to hit you, are you?" She turned her attention to Joey, who simply shook his head.

"Thanks for the offer, Winston. Maybe if I'd had the chance that day, I would have. But I get it. I've been thinkin' about what I'd do or how I'd be if Anna went missing." He clasped a hand on Winston's shoulder. "I'd probably go full psycho on a few folks, too. Don't sweat it."

Winston breathed a sigh of relief.

Anna redirected the conversation. "Would you like to come inside? Do you like toasted cheese and crackers?" She visibly cringed as soon as she asked the question. Although it was a frequent snack for her and Joey, she doubted that it was commonly served at Humbington Palace.

Grace never faltered. "That sounds delightful. May I please help you?" With that, Joey and Anna found themselves hosting the future king and queen of Taggart in their tiny, run-down home in central Idaho. Of course, two black SUVs full of SEG (Special Escort Group) soldiers idled outside.

Chapter 76

May 14, 2012

Salmon, Idaho

Midnight came and went as the two couples sat on the shabby sofa and seats, each sharing the events of the last several days from their own perspective. Simple patterned plates held the crumbs of toasted cheese and crackers that the girls had prepared. Winston took a sip from a can of root beer, which felt very American on his lips.

An invisible closeness formed as the shared experiences blended with the chemistry that is occasionally and mysteriously present between strangers.

"Oh, my! Winston, we have kept our hosts up past midnight." She turned to Joey and Anna. "Thank you so much for letting us express our gratitude and offering our apologies in person. I told Winston that I would not sleep until this was reconciled." Grace looked down in sadness. "Yet, even now, it feels so incredibly insufficient in spite of what you've done."

Grace's eyes lifted and met Joey's, which stirred his stomach. He was not interested in Grace in the slightest. She was another man's wife and he had his own. However, pleasant words from a stunning woman will have an effect. Anna looked over and was slightly puzzled to see her Joey blushing, although it did not elicit any jealousy. It still felt surreal for her to be sitting in her living room with two of the world's most famous people. She'd had friends who were huge fans of the royal family and would have gone to great lengths just to see them from a distance, maybe through a security fence as they quickly entered a limousine. They would never believe this midnight meeting even if she told them.

Grace turned to Winston and placed her hand on his knee.

"Winston!" Her eyes went wide as a bright smile crossed her face. "I've just had a splendid idea. We should have Joey and Anna to the cottage."

Winston had been in a perpetually agreeable state of mind since the previous evening and placed his hand on top of hers. "Splendid indeed." He turned to their new friends. "Is there a time that you could break away from your busy schedules to spend some time with us in the countryside?" He pronounced schedules as "sheduals." "It's quite peaceful this time of year."

Joey and Anna looked at each other with confusion. Anna asked for clarification. "Where is this cottage?" In her limited imagination, she assumed that they must own a piece of property somewhere in the western United States.

"Scullex. It's just a short hop from Morwell."

Anna's face betrayed her surprise. Was she hearing this correctly? Thankfully, her husband took the bullet and was willing to appear simple in her place. "You mean Morwell, Taggart?" he asked. "Heck. We've never been out of the country."

This only ratcheted up Grace's excitement. Her smile was now at 100%. "Then you must! This will be the experience of a lifetime. We will see to it."

Winston was also smiling and nodding enthusiastically. Constantly in his mind were the alternatives to this moment: a melancholy funeral, an empty casket, the public shame and accusations. Yes, he felt only gratitude for everyone and everything that had come together to make even this moment possible. He and Grace began planning the trip. Back and forth like a ping-pong match, they excitedly exchanged suggestions with each other.

"The Royal Pavilion!"

"Brambton Castle!"

"The Cliffs of Muldon!"

"That charming cafe' on the beach!"

"Of course!"

Anna and Joey sat with mouths open. As if the evening and their unexpected guests had not been enough, it sounded like they were now being invited to go on a vacation with royalty in Europe. As Winston and Grace sat grinning and waiting for their answer, Joey and Anna looked at each other. They had jobs and responsibilities here. They had bills to pay. The roof still needed patching. In unison, they turned toward the royal couple.

"YES!!!"

The following conversation was a flourish of plans, descriptions, questions and solutions.

"But we don't have passports."

"Diplomatic passports!"

"What about the costs?"

"You're our guests! It's the least we can do."

"But you're royalty."

"We are also people who need friends and want experiences."

Every argument was extinguished as midnight now crept past 1:00 AM.

"Winston! We've lost track of the time." Grace turned to Anna. "You have been so kind to let us invade your lovely home. We sincerely apologize for keeping you up so late. To be honest, this has been the most enjoyable time we've had with someone since..." she looked at Winston before completing the thought, "since our wedding."

He bowed his head slightly. Grace's gaze softened. "My dear Winston. Our first year together has been like a dream. However, it's been a very busy, hectic, and highly choreographed dream." She paused before continuing. "When you planned the trip to Idaho, I was so elated because it felt so...normal. It felt like what normal people do." She took his hand. "This feels normal to me. Thank you for flying halfway around the world in the middle of the night for me. It makes me love you now more than ever." With all of the emotional highs and lows of the last week, he was in a delicate state. However, as she leaned over and kissed his cheek, he radiated at her spontaneous affection. In their world, it was not always appropriate.

Winston recovered and thanked their new friends for their time. "You have been so kind. We will communicate the itinerary for our trip as soon as we return to Morwell. Please let us know if you have any needs, or wants for that matter."

Everyone stood to say goodnight when Joey spoke. "Whereabouts are you gonna spend the night tonight?"

Apparently, this small detail had not been considered in everyone's haste to get here. Winston opened his mouth but could not answer. Normally, his personal aides would have automatically handled these arrangements.

"I suppose we will find accommodations here in Salmon."

Joey spoke. "I don't mean to tell you your business, but we don't really have anywhere that you would probably stay. Salmon is a small town for tourists and anglers. You should probably just bunk here for the night."

Anna nodded approvingly.

"Bunk here?" Even the verb felt foreign on his lips.

Grace stepped in to avoid any unintentional insults. "What Winston means is that we already have imposed greatly on you. It would be too much."

"Heck, the guest bed sleeps pretty good. And if you like, we'll make you our famous biscuits and gravy in the morning. We have farm fresh eggs that are way better than what you get at the store."

Winston was at a loss. Grace was intrigued. Anna sealed the deal. "Please, it's so late and you came all this way just to check on us. Please let us do this for you."

And so the guards continued to sit for hours in the idling SUVs. Two rotated perimeter duty every two hours as the others slept. It would be a long night, but nothing unusual for their breed. Their moods and attitudes softened even more when Anna appeared at 8:00 AM with a tray of fresh breakfast for everyone. Idaho was kind to its visitors.

Chapter 77
May 14, 2012
Hwy 21, Idaho

The rented Chevy Malibu was constantly weaving within its lane and occasionally drifting across the lines to its right and left. As the right tires left the pavement, sending up a cloud of dust, Chester dropped his notepad and grabbed the steering wheel. After landing in Boise two hours earlier, he had picked up his car and grabbed a donut and some coffee before heading northeast toward Salmon. The clerk at the rental car window had gushed about the beauty of the route he would be taking. He had provided a map and was enthusiastically circling scenic spots along the highway adding "You have GOT to check this out" with each one. After the fifth circle, Chester grabbed the map and offered an insincere "Thank you!" as he headed toward the lot.

Now, over an hour into his journey, he was detesting the scenic highway. It twisted, turned, rose and fell with the rugged Idaho topography. Precipitous drop offs to his right constantly threatened to turn him (and his car) into a Missing Person Report at every bend. It was difficult enough to make calls on his cell phone, scribble notes in his notepad, and try to eat breakfast without having to maneuver through nature's obstacle course.

Despite his irritation, he spoke in a friendly tone as he made his next phone call.

"Achak! How's it going, buddy?"

The reply was oddly and expectedly flat. "I'm well."

"Yeah, I just landed and wanted to make sure you're still up to play tour guide today. Got your camera ready?" Chester's tone was jovial and almost patronizing.

"Yes. It is ready, as am I." No emotion, one tone.

"Great! Looks like I should be there around noon if I don't accidentally drive off into one of these canyons." Chester laughed but it was not returned.

"Alright, Achak. See ya' soon, bud!" He pressed End and then quickly jerked the wheel as tires screeched in protest. Small pieces of gravel kicked up from the shoulder tumbled hundreds of feet into the seemingly bottomless ravine.

Chapter 78

May 14, 2012

Morwell, Taggart

Another shift began like most others. Olivia checked her email and looked at the previous shift's duty log. At every entry, the simple acronym NSTR indicated that there was Nothing Significant To Report. Although she enjoyed the intermittent anomalies and their associated challenges, she was content to keep the digital world neat and tidy today. In her mind, it was almost like gardening. She knew there were rabbits and crows and weasels out there who would love nothing more than to have free reign of Taggart's digital produce. *Not on my watch,* she thought as she imagined herself dressed like a shotgun-wielding farmer checking the fence line to make sure there were no gaps or weak points.

It was about 10:00 AM. She began to type a random command into a program when the keyboard suddenly went dead. She frowned and tried a few more keys but there was no response – same with the mouse. Questioning grunts and loud key strikes from her coworkers caused her to look left and right. This made no sense. How could everyone simultaneously have a hardware problem? The realization of this impossibility quickly pulled her attention back to the screen. She was staring at it when her cursor suddenly moved on its own as if someone had remotely accessed her computer. It was only about a quarter inch, but her heart froze. It was unthinkable. TI-7 was a closed loop with impenetrable firewalls, or so she thought.

Her eyes frantically scanned her workstation, her peers and the room but everyone seemed more frustrated than concerned. She could hear her heart pounding in her ears when the screen flickered and everything returned to normal. Everyone else in the room muttered and went back to work. Cautiously, she refrained from touching anything and slid her roller chair away from her workstation. As she walked toward her supervisor's desk, she began to question if she'd actually seen what she thought she did. After all, no one else seemed alarmed. But she was the Bloodhound. She had not chosen this name. It had been given to her – awarded, you might say. Moments like this and her intuition were the reasons why.

Chapter 79

May 14, 2012

Salmon, Idaho

The rented Malibu drove aimlessly through the streets of Salmon. Achak sat in the passenger seat with his camera sitting in his lap. He looked placid and unconcerned.

Chester, however, tried not to reveal his irritation. The redeye flight, harrowing drive and obscurity of this small town caused him to be edgy. Sitting beside this stoically silent Native American, he cursed himself for not having access to an actual private investigator.

They turned into the Sip-N-Shake as Chester stopped the car and scanned the mostly closed businesses around them. He wasn't even sure what he was looking for. His frustration continued to build and spilled out just a little as he turned to Achak and said, "Not much action in this sleepy little town." As expected, Achak appeared completely oblivious to the quip and Chester's derision.

He sat there, questioning his instincts. Normally, they led him down the right path directly behind his prey. Was he slipping? Had the shutdown of his website rattled him more than he'd realized? Was the idea of revenge clouding his logic? He continued to brood as his hatred of Idaho continued to simmer like a restless volcano. That's when he saw it, or more accurately, them.

For the first time, Achak showed genuine surprise. Without warning, the Malibu went into gear and the front tires barked as they accelerated away from the Sip-N-Shake. He held tightly to his camera with one hand and grasped wildly for the handle on the passenger door. Instead of entering the street at an exit, the Malibu cleared the curb at a fairly high speed. Sparks flew as the radiator supports struck asphalt. The rear end fishtailed as Chester continued to accelerate behind two black SUVs that were heading south on Main Street toward Highway 93.

"Get it! Shots! We need shots!" Chester was yelling as the Malibu began to close the gap. Achak's face was ashen as he robotically raised the camera to his eye and began to press the shutter button.

"Close ups!" shouted Chester. Achak tried his best to manipulate the long lens as his body shifted side to side in the careening vehicle. About 100 yards back, Chester slowed to normal speeds and barked, "Drop the camera." Achak obeyed. "Just act normal. Be cool."

The Malibu did its best to blend in, but the empty

highway did little to conceal its proximity. The two black SUVs turned right onto Highway 93 and then slowed as they neared the sign for Lemhi County Airport.

"I knew it," Chester seethed through clenched teeth. As the two SUVs turned, the Malibu continued driving south as casually as a car could.

Achak turned around out of curiosity before Chester spat "Don't look! Eyes straight ahead." He quickly spun back forward and complied as he began to wonder if he had gotten into the car with a psycho. As the airport entrance disappeared from view, Chester swung the car around with squealing tires. Gravel was flung as he accelerated back to the north a few hundred yards and then quickly stopped on the shoulder. "Camera!" he demanded, holding out his right hand without taking his eyes off the airport.

He grabbed the camera and expertly held it in place as he targeted his quarry. He snapped a few shots with the lens zoomed in. At this distance, the naked eye could only discern the vague outline of vehicles. Then, Chester set the camera down and shifted the car into Drive. He sat with his left foot on the brake and his right hovering over the gas pedal. His eyes were unblinkingly fixed on some distant object.

Suddenly, the feet switched position and the Malibu once again shot forward as it re-entered the highway. Achak's eyes were wide with fear as the V-6 engine screamed with exertion. At the airport entrance, Chester jerked the wheel to the right as the car leaned precariously on the edge of traction. Although they were separated by a chain link security fence, the distance between the vehicles was now less than 200 yards. Achak braced himself as he expected that his crazed driver was about to ram the gate. His body was thrown forward against the seatbelt as the nose of Malibu dove with extreme braking. Chester was instantly out of the car, camera raised and snapping constantly in the newly formed cloud of dust. The maneuver apparently had its desired effect because doors of the rear SUV swung open as guards exited and raised short black rifles toward the sedan. Two other guards were smothering two other figures with their bodies and hustling them toward the open door of a waiting private jet. The camera clicked over and over. The tail-mounted engines raised in pitch and began to push the aircraft forward even as the door was pulled shut. The guards retreated to the opposite side of the SUV as their gun barrels began to peer out from around its edges. Within two minutes, the private jet was accelerating down the runway and lifting off into a beautiful blue sky. Achak was tucked into a ball in the passenger floorboard, eyes wide with distress. Chester slowly lowered the camera. He was beaming.

Chapter 80

May 14, 2012

Morwell, Taggart

Bancroft bent at the waist as he poured the tea into the waiting ivory cup that sat on the silver tray. The Queen was giving him a most disapproving gaze, which he continued to evade. He concluded the pour, set down the silver kettle and asked, "Will there be anything else, your Highness?" He stood ramrod straight and continued to stare forward.

"Your avoidance will not outlast my determination."

Bancroft's eyes had no option but to concede as he finally looked at her.

"Don't think that you are my only source of information, Bancroft. I've been made aware of their subsequent hasty departure. If you know something of this globetrotting business, it would be in your best interest to divulge it immediately."

He'd known the Queen for long enough to discern her

ire. His allegiance to Winston had its limits.

"They've returned to Idaho. It was done with great haste. I assume it is with regards to their recent foray."

The Queen looked appalled. "Dreadful business, this gallivanting about. I told you that no good would come of this." Although those actual words had not been spoken, Bancroft humbly acknowledged that it was true.

"Yes, your Highness." Although he was a fixture at the palace and carried some influence because of his position, Bancroft also understood that royal living could take its toll. Inwardly, he admired Winston and Grace for "coloring outside of the lines" in their youth. He felt it was good for their sanity. Rarely seen by anyone, his lips spread into the faintest of grins.

"I see that, Bancroft. I am not amused."

Chapter 81

May 14, 2012

Morwell, Taggart

This was the second anomaly of the day. Earlier, there had been the ubiquitous disturbance of the computer network. Now, she was being called in after hours. Although it was always a possible requirement of her duties, she had never been summoned in such an urgent manner. Checking back into the secure facility, she felt like she had accidentally arrived at the wrong address. Instead of smart business attire, her coworkers as well as her supervisor looked absurdly casual. The ladies wore no makeup and most everyone was adorned in some variety of t-shirt. One of the male techs was wearing pajama pants.

Mallory, her supervisor, spoke. "We have a Level Two breach. At around 5:00 PM local time, 7:00 AM Mountain time, the Item experienced an unforeseen exposure."

Olivia was baffled by this news. The "Item" was the

code which referred to Winston and Grace when they were appearing together. Thinking back to her high school geography lessons, she recalled that the Mountain time zone was in the western portion of the United States. She had always considered it the most majestic of time zones.

Mallory continued. "The Item was attempting to depart from a rural airstrip in Salmon, Idaho when two men in a vehicle drew near and began to take photographs. The men have been identified by the local law enforcement." Mallory turned as the faces of two men appeared on one of the screens affixed to the wall behind her. The second was a dark-skinned man by the name of Achak Strong Runner: Native American, age 34, resident of Salmon Idaho. No criminal history. One traffic violation for Expired License Plate and a credit score of 760. The first man, however, was known to Olivia. Her lip involuntarily lifted into a slight snarl at the sight of him.

Chester Wade Hannigan, age 35, resident of Chicago, Illinois. His criminal history was fairly lengthy with multiple trespassing charges, one for stalking and multiple active restraining orders. His traffic violations were just as numerous with a litany of speeding tickets. The data of infractions and nefarious associations scrolled in a loop on the screen. Oliva continued to scowl at the sight of her newest nemesis. She had been responsible for sending the bug that wiped out his website, and she interpreted his involvement as a blatant attempt at revenge. Being Taggish and part of TI-7, she couldn't help but feel moral superiority to this miscreant.

Although diminutive in size and meek in demeanor, a dangerous fire began to burn in her gut. Her jaw flexed as she ran through a laundry list of potential digital attacks that she could launch. Then, she recalled the glitch from this morning. Chester Hannigan did not seem capable of high-level hacking. No. He was a brute, an opportunist. Either the two incidents were not related or there was an accomplice.

Chapter 82

May 17, 2012

Salmon, Idaho

Anna turned off the highway onto the familiar dirt drive. All week long, she'd felt as if she would burst with the secret of her new friendship. At every encounter with friends and coworkers, it was so difficult to keep from blurting out that Winston and Grace had spent the night in their home and that they were now planning a vacation together. Of course, everyone would have thought she had somehow become an eight-year-old girl making up fairy tales. But it had happened, right? It wasn't just a dream – the knock on the door, the breakfast, the plea for absolute secrecy.

Before leaving, Winston and Grace explained that an enormous amount of "burdensome discretion" would be required in their relationship. They described how merciless the news and tabloids could be and that they would not wish that type of treatment for anyone they truly cared about. Although it was difficult to conceal, it was also incredibly exciting. It felt not only exciting but even dangerous.

For the last several years, Anna had halfheartedly been praying that their lives would take some unexpected turn. A fear had settled into her heart that they would always be stuck in Salmon, growing overly content and unusually quiet. She envisioned a future version of themselves, sitting across from each other in the booth of a diner, not smiling, not talking, just existing. The mental picture made her shiver. But that impossible prayer had been answered!

She thought back over the crazy turn of events and could not help but smile. When things seemed at the point of permanently breaking, Joey came home from his camping trip with a bruised eye and crazy story. Even the uncertainty of that had been transformed into something amazing. In some strange, revelatory sense, even their challenges seemed to be serving some purpose. She thought back to a saying of her father's: "Water tastes best when you need it most."

She walked to the mailbox and was puzzled to see a large, ornate envelope addressed to Mr. and Mrs. Joey Woodford. It had no return address but had a large "overnight" postage sticker that looked unfamiliar to her. She wanted to rip it open right on the spot to see what mysterious treasure it might contain but, no. She wanted to wait on Joey. He would be home soon.

Chapter 83

May 17, 2012

Salmon, Idaho

Scott Olens was also deep in thought as he drove home from his last vet appointment. Country music played softly through the speakers of his pickup as he rested his left cheek against his fist, his left elbow propped near the open window. He'd run into Joey again today and the guy was completely different somehow. You could just sense it on him and around him. In place of confusion, he looked calm. In place of worry, he looked peaceful. However, he'd been slightly elusive when asked about it.

"It's been a strange few weeks, Scott. I've been about as low as you can go and about as high as a man can be while he's sober."

The statement helped to assuage some suspicions or concerns that had crept into Scott's thoughts. "Anything in particular?" he ventured to ask.

Joey thought before answering. "Things have been happening. I don't really understand it. A few weeks ago, I thought the world was falling apart. I wasn't feeling good about a lot of things: work, money, my marriage, the future. Now, it's like a storm blew past and the sun is peeking out. But it's more than that. It feels like something good is happening. I feel like I did when I was a kid and I knew my birthday was coming up. It just feels like someone is really doing me a solid."

The answer only puzzled Scott more but he was thankful to see his friend in better spirits. He thought of a verse in Romans where it says to "Rejoice with those who rejoice, weep with those who weep." Life seems to give more of the latter than the former, so he tried to take advantage of the good moments.

"I'm really glad to hear that, Joey. I was worried about you a while back. You need anything?

"Maybe. Not right now but maybe soon. When I do, I'll remember that you offered."

Chapter 84

May 17, 2012

Salmon, Idaho

The unopened envelope sat there on their kitchen table. Anna and Joey stood beside each other, looking at it reverently as if its contents would change their lives forever. Neither spoke, but they grinned at each other. Without needing instruction, they quickly spread about the room where the lock was checked and the curtains were closed. Silently, they reconvened at the table.

"You ready?" he asked. Anna nodded.

He whipped open the folding knife that was always clipped to his right jean pocket. As he moved in to begin the procedure, she put her hands out and offered a helpful "Easy."

Their eyes met briefly before he carefully sliced through the end and gently let the contents slide out onto their well-worn table. Two leather wallets adorned with gold leaf crests were on top of multiple documents. The pages were printed on expensive tinted stationary with a similar gold leaf letterhead. The cover letter was addressed to them.

Joey and Anna,

We will be delighted to accept you into our beloved Taggart on the 26th of May. Transportation has been arranged and will be available from your address of record to the aforementioned destination. You will be departing on Friday, May 25th at 5:00 pm. Peter, one of our staff, will accompany you as your assistant. Should you think of anything that will improve your holiday, please do not hesitate to ask. We've been apprised of your contribution to the Royal family and intend to display the full magnitude of our gratitude.

In Your Service,
Amanda Hughes
Secretary of Social Affairs

Anna threw her arms around Joey, squealed and planted a big kiss right on his lips. He thought pleasantly to himself, *When was the last time you earned one of those?* Joey rarely allowed himself any credit. It wasn't in him to seek the spotlight or recognition. This time, however, he let himself recall those days on the plateau:

the leap off the cliff, the rescue, the long trudge out. At the time, he didn't understand why he had gone through all of that but now, there seemed to be some higher purpose taking place. It made him question all of the challenges in his life – past, present and future. It introduced the possibility that maybe it wasn't all meaningless chance. Maybe his life mattered. Maybe his marriage mattered. Maybe his innermost hopes and desires were important to somebody. Maybe Scott wasn't as far out there as he had once thought.

Chapter 85

May 17, 2012

Unknown Location

Spyder's hands flew over the keyboard as the continual tapping of keys caused strings of seemingly random numbers to appear on the screen. It was a program that had been affectionately named The Leech. Like the actual parasite, it could attach itself without alerting its victim. A blood thinning serum was then injected, which allowed the desired medium to flow freely. It would only be the attention of another who would eventually point out the bloated, gorged fiend attached to some obscure part of the body. Then, in full panic, the victim would try to detach the slimy, slippery appendage but with no success, for the head sucker would be firmly implanted.

Tempting as it was to dispatch The Leech just out of amusement, Spyder waited. The most recent client had requested that it occur when he wanted it to. Apparently,

Chester was working on a surprise of his own.

Chapter 86

May 18, 2012

Chicago, Illinois

With an abundance of caution, Chester had unplugged every external connection from his computers except for the power cords. Without attachment to the World Wide Web, he felt fairly safe editing the photos that he had downloaded from Achak's camera. Although no faces could be discerned, they were very compelling. Anyone who had ever seen the royal couple could match their general body shapes and features, even from behind. The two of them together with the private plane and royal guards in the background were way more convincing than other photos he'd posted in the past. He used an editing program to attach the pictures in the sequence so that they formed a staccato cartoon. It showed the couple being whisked into the jet by two guards who, by their clothing and mannerisms, looked very Taggish.

He pondered how a country so closely related to the United States could still be oceans apart, both literally and figuratively.

Chester had always harbored a grudge against any type of aristocracy. *They put their pants on one leg at a time just like the rest of us,* he often reminded himself. However, in his imagination, the pants were being held by some poor servant. It disgusted him. He was baffled that anyone could arbitrarily declare themselves superior to others and stupefied that everyone else would just go along with it. It made no sense. Just like the Caesars of Rome trying to convince everyone that they were gods, he couldn't believe the utter foolishness of it all. *Everyone is going to worship something,* he thought to himself. Well, Chester would worship Chester. And if Chester could offer Chester a Rolex or a Porsche or a beautiful woman or money, he would gladly lay down his offering at his own self-serving throne.

Chapter 87
May 25, 2012
Salmon, Idaho

At 4:55 PM, Anna and Joey sat low in the cushions of their couch with two pieces of luggage sitting to their right and left. His leg bounced nervously and she looked at the clock for the tenth time. Neither spoke because they didn't want anything to disrupt their rapt attention to the driveway. The bouncing stopped and they both cocked their heads as the sound of gravel crunching outside told their ears that someone had just turned off the highway. Like kids, they ran to the window and peeked through the curtains to see two black SUVs approaching.

"Just play it cool," he reassured her with a smile. They were almost dancing in place as they heard doors open and footsteps approach. Before the third knock even sounded, they opened their door as ceremoniously as possible and stood hip to hip, smiling broadly at whoever had arrived.

A pleasant young man, pale and thin, greeted them with a snaggle tooth smile. He was dressed smartly in a black suit.

"Mr. and Mrs. Woodford, I presume?"

Joey shot out his hand. "I'm Joey and this is Anna. We're the Woodfords." He couldn't entirely conceal his nervous excitement. "Joey and Anna Woodford," he slowly repeated with exaggeration.

"I am Peter Smelling, aid to Her Majesty. I will be serving as your personal assistant for the next few days. May I take your luggage?" His smile was so earnest and he seemed so eager to please that they accepted his offer.

Awkwardly, he wrestled the heavy bags outside and loaded them into the back of one of the vehicles. He then hurriedly opened the rear passenger door for Anna and ran around to open Joey's. At each occasion, he would almost snap to attention and offer his quirky smile like a bellhop eager for a tip.

Inside the vehicle was a bottle of champagne with a hand-written note attached to its neck:

Adventure awaits! No rescues needed this time (we hope!). W & G

There was also a wicker basket full of packaged nuts and cookies. They both noted that they were foreign selections that you would probably never see at the local grocery store. The SUVs pulled onto the highway and made the short trip to the local airport where a private jet sat waiting on the tarmac. There was no parking deck, no TSA, no metal detectors. An attractive female dressed in a well-fitting blue skirt and blouse exited the steps and greeted them by name as she welcomed them aboard. Once seated in the leather and mahogany seats, their attendant offered them sleep masks and ear plugs. The engines powered up and, for the first time in their lives, they began to travel eastward across the pond.

Chapter 88

May 26, 2012

Morwell, Taggart

Normally, working on a Saturday would have been an extreme annoyance, even degrading. Adamantly, the smug side of her relegated people who worked weekends and swing shifts as those who had typically not applied themselves in life. This, however, was different. Oliva was "essential personnel" and her unit was facing a crisis. The reputation and honor of the crown was at stake. With the appearance of Chester on their radar twice this month, the situation threat level had been elevated, which meant twenty-four-hour sentry duty for her and the other technicians. Dutifully, they rotated shifts and perpetually monitored the various websites, news channels and tabloids. Nothing out of the ordinary had surfaced. They were fairly certain that photos had been taken of the Item although none of them had been posted, yet.

Olivia had become comfortable working again, and every hour that passed with her computer responding properly felt like gaining distance from whatever or whoever had tested their defenses. Still, the nagging uneasiness remained in the corner of her mind.

Chapter 89
May 26, 2012
Chicago, Illinois

The cell phone rang with a familiar number. Chester quickly constructed his strategy for the negotiation and put on his game face.

"'Ello, gov'ner'" the voice with the heavy Kenkly accent greeted.

"What have you got?" Chester asked with as little emotion as he could convey.

"Now, now, mate. No 'ello? No how ya' doin?"

Chester remained silent on his end. It was all part of the game.

"Ah-right, Ah-right. I got sometin' good for ya' dis time. More than two-grand good if you catch my drift."

"Two-grand is good money for a thirty-second phone call. What is that, like $240,000 an hour by my math."

"The phone call is just 'da tip of 'de iceberg. We both know there's a lot more in front and behind what I gots to say."

The analogy didn't make complete sense to Chester, but he continued anyway.

"I'm waiting."

"It's dem lovebirds again. Been hopping the pond a lot quite lately."

"This isn't news. I saw them myself. I've got photos of them taking off."

"But now they ain't alone."

Chester was truly surprised by this, though he disciplined himself to wait in silence for his contact to continue.

"Got a look at a flight manifest. Leaving Hedgerow with four passengers but coming back with six."

"When?" Chester asked cooly.

"That depends. I'm thinkin' five grand this time around."

"This could be useless or old news. This could be the flight I saw take off."

"You didn't see this one take off unless you was just at the airport."

His contact has slipped up and accidentally revealed the timeline. Chester was tempted to hang up and run with the info, but this informant might be useful in the future. No sense in burning bridges to save a few thousand.

"Tell you what, I'll pay three and if you can offer any intel from your end when they land, I'll make it five."

"You drive a hard bargin', you stingy ol' Scrooge. I'll sees what I can see."

The call ended and Chester placed a call to the airline.

"I need your next flight out to Morwell."

Chapter 90

May 26, 2012

Morwell, Taggart

When Anna's eyes opened, she smiled at the realization of where she was. Normally, flying east can cause some serious jet lag but she had slept a deep sleep full of pleasant dreams. Maybe it was the in-flight meal. Maybe it was the amazingly soft sheets and blankets. Maybe it was the rich scent of fine leather. Whatever it was, she possessed a peculiar sense of hope and expectation. They were feelings she had not felt with this intensity since childhood. It felt like Christmas.

Joey's face was less than a foot away. Instead of the distant, pained expression she'd grown to expect, his face was wearing a silly grin.

"I trust your highness slept well last night," he said with a truly horrendous Taggish accent. Anna crackled, which was like music to his ears. *How did this happen?*

he asked himself. Just a few weeks ago, life felt like a prison that he'd somehow constructed around himself. Now, it felt like he'd won the lottery. Not necessarily a lottery of money but of fulfillment, joy and excitement. Everything felt new: his marriage, his outlook, his potential.

A pleasant female voice with an actual Taggish accent sounded over the private plane's intercom system.

"Passengers, we will be landing in approximately twenty minutes. I will be visiting the cabin to assist you shortly."

"Shall we adorn ourselves for the day's endeavor?" he asked again with that awful accent.

Anna was holding her stomach from laughter. "Stop it! That doesn't even make any sense. Day's endeavor?" The love he had for her also felt renewed.

The royal treatment continued as the jet landed and taxied to the area for private aviation. As the door opened, a short red carpet led to an immaculate Range Rover with tiny flags mounted at the front of the hood. Peter was somehow already stationed at the open rear door with his patented disheveled smile. Joey and Anna both felt as if they'd knocked on the wrong door and arrived at the wrong house.

"This can't all be for us," she leaned over and whispered to Joey.

He, on the other hand, was taking full advantage of the moment. He was waving to imaginary crowds and using that horrific accent again. "Lay-ees and gent-el-men, please welcome The Beat-els!"

Anna elbowed him in the ribs, but he could tell she was loving it. She was loving the new him.

As they entered the luxury SUV, Peter turned around and announced from the front seat, "I've taken the liberty of selecting your breakfast: curry porridge with black pudding and mushrooms."

Peter remained serious as long as he could before bursting out into laughter. "I'm sorry but you should have seen your faces." He wiped a tear from his eye. "Actually, there is a basket of warm scones and a thermos of tea. If it is not to your liking, I believe the Duke and Duchess have arranged brunch at the cottage."

The Taggish countryside did not disappoint. Although Idaho had its own unique splendor, it did not have the lush green hills and charming, picturesque villages. Anna realized with horror that she was smudging the inside of the glass as she pressed her face against it to take it all in. Part of her thought that some cleaning crew would sweep in immediately after they exited the vehicle to prepare it for its next errand. However, she wasn't yet comfortable with the thought of having "servants."

Chapter 91

May 26, 2012

Morwell, Taggart

Transatlantic flights were the worst. Since it was a last-minute work trip, Chester ended up sitting in the last row near the latrine. All night long, the bathroom door opened and shut with a blinding light that scorched his eyes each time. A fussy baby sat in the row ahead who must have been affected by the pressure because it cried for what seemed like ten hours straight. Add in the only seats on the plane that don't recline and the with the delight scent of sewage, he was truly in last class.

His eyes felt like someone had poured sand inside of his eyelids as he made his way through customs and then to the rental car counter. Ignoring the pleasantries of the clerk, he took his keys to an economy level Peugeot and absentmindedly entered the left side of the car. It took a while for his foggy mind to understand why the steering wheel was on the right side. Cursing under his breath, he exited and walked around to the other side.

He'd driven in Taggart before, but it was when he'd been better rested. Today, he was the target of much horn blowing and shaking fists as he awkwardly negotiated each intersection and traffic circle. It felt like riding a bicycle with your arms crossed.

As he drove away from the airport, he called his contact.

"Mornin' gov-nor!" came the chirped greeting. It was grating in Chester's ears.

"Where are they?" His tone was sour and flat.

"Hea'ed south. Black Range Rover, no escort, diploma'ic flag."

"Any idea where they're headed?"

"I'm guessin' the royal cott-age."

"Where's that?"

"Scullex. Down where all the fancy pants be livin'."

Chapter 92

26 May 2012,

Scullex, Taggart

If the drive down from Morwell had been spectacular, what awaited them was a veritable paradise. The SUV slowed and turned down a remote country lane. It began to run beside an incredibly long row of thick vegetation. Eventually, it slowed and turned into an alcove where there was a heavy security gate, booth and armed guards. The gate opened as the attending sentry snapped a sharp palm-open salute.

Once inside, nothing was out of place. Joey and Anna moved their heads from one window to another as they tried to take in every detail. Blend together the botanical gardens, the fountains of Rome, an architect from Disney and you have the royal cottage. Looking at the flawless lawn, Joey imagined a scissor-wielding servant whose job was to dart out of his one-man shed and quickly trim any stray blades that he noticed.

As they rounded the circular cobblestone drive, they stopped perfectly in front of an intricately manicured sidewalk. Waiting on the front porch were their hosts. Winston and Grace looked as if they'd stepped out of a fashion magazine. Each wore well-fitting jeans and sweaters with collared shirts showing at the neck. They strolled from the cottage, arm in arm, smiling with their patented charm. As the two Yankee visitors were let out of the vehicle, Grace wrapped Anna in a hug that was somehow both formal and affectionate. Joey and Winston shook hands and appeared as men who mutually respected each other.

"Some place you got here," Joey offered, smiling more than he had in years.

"Yes, it's a wonderful respite from the hustle and bustle," Winston responded. "I suppose you enjoy this type of tranquility all the time in Idaho."

Joey wrinkled his face to acknowledge the loose parallel. "All this place needs is the scent of cow poop."

Anna looked mortified, but Winston thought it was hilarious. Grace covered her mouth to suppress a giggle. It was odd chemistry but it somehow worked. The foursome fell into easy conversation and a comfortable presence as if they'd known each other for years. The strong emotions that surrounded their introduction (or intrusion) into each other's lives had accelerated the process of familiarization.

The rest of the day was spent enjoying the pool,

trying out the tennis courts and, of course, constantly snacking on treats supplied by the kitchen staff. When Joey and Anna asked if they were going to venture into the countryside, Winston and Grace exchanged glances and replied with a small amount of mischief, "We've allowed you to rest this afternoon in preparation for tomorrow's adventures. You're going to need it."

Chapter 93

May 26, 2012

Scullex, Taggart

His mind was just not operating correctly. Almost forty-eight hours without genuine sleep and the difference of six time zones had zapped Chester's alertness. Even though it was broad daylight, he found himself drifting dangerously across the centerline and occasionally off the shoulder. If he were going to die young, he would have imagined being shot by a security guard or eaten by a vicious guard dog. However, the entire last week of close calls introduced the possibility of dying behind the wheel.

His contact's spotty directions coupled with his sleep deprivation made navigating in the Taggish countryside a very frustrating task. It was dumb luck that he turned right onto a remote country lane when armed guards seemed to materialize from the hedges. Wide-eyed, Chester slammed on the brakes and stopped as one circled to the driver's window as the other casually held the rifle across his chest.

"State your business," came the terse demand.

He tried his best to play dumb. "Ahh, shucks. I think I got turned around. I was looking for Tall Tim and somehow ended up way out here. Is this Humbington?"

The guard sneered slightly at yet another "stupid American tourist." Chester must have been convincing because he was quickly dismissed instead of being interrogated.

"Bug off, wanker. Private property of the Queen."

Jackpot! Chester thought without revealing his pleasure.

"Sorry, bud." Chester leaned his head out, looked around and asked innocently. "Say, is she here? Man, it'd be cool to get an autograph or maybe even a selfie." Chester pulled out an American five-dollar bill and looked around again before slowly moving it towards the guard.

If the solider was perturbed before, he was downright disgusted now. His sneer became a full-blown scowl as he barked "Clear out, now! Private property!" The other guard raised his rifle ever so slightly.

Chester didn't want to press his luck, although he had enjoyed pushing their buttons. Grinding the gears, he found reverse and slowly departed the seclusive compound.

For now.

Chapter 94

May 26, 2012

Scullex, Taggart

The day was absolutely magnificent. Being outside of the United States is interesting because lungs, eyes, ears, the tongue and nose all function the same. However, their sensations are new, usually in a subtle way but the combined experience can be profound. This was the case for Joey and especially Anna. Her mind and body had been thirsting for inspiration for quite some time. To escape from the drudgeries of everyday life in such a splendid fashion was infusing life into her weary soul. Each bite of a new food, breath of cool humid air and every syllable of the delightful dialect that fell on her ear made her feel alive in a way that had almost been forgotten.

Joey found himself enjoying a new inner rhythm. Back at home, life had felt like trudging through mud, making little progress and wondering what was the point of it all. However, the recent turn of events had ignited a desire within himself to surrender to change. Although he couldn't fully explain it, he felt like he'd been fighting a current only to realize that it would eventually take him to a pleasant place if he could let it.

Winston and Grace were also receiving a huge dose of refreshment. First of all, just being alive and together was a perpetual spring of gratefulness. The company, however, was an unexpected catalyst. This high school educated, blue collar, low to middle class couple from Idaho did not require formality or etiquette. Instead of perfect posture and carefully watched words, Grace found herself barefoot and slumped against Winston on a wicker couch that was arranged around a fire pit. After a delectable dinner of pheasant, grilled asparagus, and baked Jersey Royals, the couples had gathered on the back patio where they had made s'mores. The conversation flowed easily as each told tales of childhood coupled with hopes and dreams of the future. Winston and Grace were mischievously vague about their itinerary for the next day and grinned like Cheshire cats with their secret knowledge.

Chapter 95

May 27, 2012

Scullex, Taggart

Chester's eyes were as red as his head was foggy. The jet lag and sleep deprivation were clouding his decision-making abilities and yet he persisted. He was siphoning from his tank of anger to supplement his bone-dry tank of rest. Whenever he felt tempted to lean his seat back and catch some much-needed shut eye, he thought of the aloof and untouchable royal family and how they had nuked his website. He saw himself as a soldier and a nationalist. They had attacked his personal Pearl Harbor and he had retaliated by declaring war. Although he had never served in the military and wasn't really comfortable outdoors, he knew that nighttime was when an enemy was most vulnerable.

Camera in hand, he snuck through the field and could see the dense hedgerow looming stalwartly in the moonlight. Cautiously, he crept up on his hands and knees, expecting flood lights and barking dogs at any second. He felt a small sense of victory as he drew near without incident. His plan was to squeeze through the hedge, find a good vantage point inside of the compound and snap away when the fancy-pants couple and their new chums drag themselves out of bed sometime the next morning. They would be exclusive shots that his audience would pay through the nose to see. He reminded himself to adjust his subscription rates when he got back to Chicago.

Perhaps it was his current state of alertness (or lack thereof) that prevented him from hearing the faint buzz. Had he approached in the daytime, he would have seen the warnings posted at set intervals along the hedge. "Warning! Electric Fence. Private Property. Do Not Enter." Chester stuck a hand through the hedge and inwardly scoffed at this shoddy expectation of security. He was pushing his head through and was up to his chest in branches when he reached for something to pull himself further in.

WASP! FIRE! SNAKE BITE! were the alarms sounding in his mind. It only lasted a second, but the jolt contracted every muscle in his body and made him let out a yelp that was both fearful and childish in its tone. In full blown panic, he scrambled backwards out of the hedge as floodlights erupted around the entire perimeter of the complex. Stumbling to his feet, Chester was running away across the field. He tripped and crashed onto the ground, which was thankfully covered in tall grass. Immediately, he was up and running again. With great relief, he realized he was still holding onto his camera. To assuage this momentary defeat, he encouraged himself with the thought that a good soldier never leaves his rifle.

Chapter 96

May 27, 2012

Scullex, Taggart

Winston and Grace were acting like school children during breakfast. As Joey and Anna enjoyed their full gourmet English breakfast, their new friends squirmed in their seats and were caught more than once looking out toward the horizons.

"What are you guys up to?" Anna asked.

Grace stifled a grin as she replied, "We're just excited to show you the countryside."

Anna and Joey were right to be suspicious. As the plates were taken away, a distant thumping sound was heard by all. The sound grew louder and louder until a large maroon helicopter shot over the cottage just above the tree line at high speeds.

Winston and Grace jumped out of their seats and thrust their hands into the air in triumph. "TA DA!!!" they both shouted.

Anna and Joey were crouched low, feeling like World War III had just started. The helicopter rose and banked dramatically in the sky before turning around and setting down within the fence line on a marked pad. Bits of grass clippings swirled in the air and then settled as the powerful turbine spun down. Two guards and faithful Peter exited with their heads lowered as the blades of the Sikorsky S-76C continued to slow.

Winston and Grace were giddy with excitement. Almost in perfect unison, they announced, "We're taking the helicopter!" Although this was not a new experience for the royal couple, they were thrilled to be able to offer this to their new friends. Neither Joey nor Anna had ever been in one.

The interior was every bit as plush as the private jet. Once inside, each put on headsets that allowed them to talk to one another and hear announcements from the pilot. It was yet another new and novel sensation as the collective was pulled up and the aircraft began to defy gravity. Faces were pressed against the window as the pilot pointed out various castles, farms and towns. Joey noted that very little detracted from the view. There were no gaudy billboards, huge parking lots or golden arches – just pristine countryside. He marveled at how this smaller country had been preserved for thousands of years and, in some ways, America had become a little cluttered in just over two hundred.

Up ahead, the green horizon seemed to end suddenly

with no explanation. The aircraft dropped low and skimmed just above the roofs of houses when the ground beneath them disappeared and was replaced with white capped water. They banked left and saw tall white cliffs that formed a menacing boundary for the restless waves which broke against their base.

"The world-famous Cliffs of Muldon," the pilot announced. The passengers strained to see outside of the small window. Anna and Joey squeezed each other's hands and smiled at the shared experience of seeing this in person.

"Are those sailboats?" Joey asked, looking down at the sea (which was actually the Taggish Channel). "I've always wanted to try that."

Winston responded with a glint in his eye. "Well, you're in luck, my friend." The Sikorsky rose gently toward the top of the cliff when the landing gear clunked open and locked into position.

Chapter 97

May 27, 2012

Scullex, Taggart

The sound of the low flying helicopter startled Chester as he slept in the front seat of his rented Peugeot. Groggily, he rubbed his eyes and squinted at the gleaming maroon aircraft flying toward the compound.

"Jackpot," he said to himself. He drank the cold coffee that remained in a Styrofoam cup in his console and ate a few biscuits (or as Americans would say, airline cookies). Minutes later, as the helicopter took off, he shifted into first and did his best to follow its general course. Navigating by sight and instinct, he found himself near the shore. After about thirty minutes, the large aircraft set down just beyond some nearby trees. Chester didn't see a road that would get him any closer, so he grabbed his camera and set out on foot.

Still feeling the effects from the horrible flight, he was running on fumes, or possibly just greed and revenge. Panting with exertion, he broke through the trees just as the doors to a black SUV were closing. Instinctively, he raised the camera and grabbed a few shots that he knew were worthless without discernible faces. Only the hack jobs and second-rate tabloids posted photos without any substance. No. He was no chump. The perfect shot – the coup de grace was waiting. He just needed patience and persistence. After the chopper departed, he wearily jogged and sometimes walked down the country road where the SUV had traveled.

Chapter 98
May 27, 2012
Scullex, Taggart

The guards remained at a distance the entire time but could be seen boarding a small motorboat at the other end of the pier.

Winston placed a low profile, self-inflating PFD around his neck before adorning his head with a white Captain's hat.

Grace rolled her eyes and asked, "You're not actually going to wear that silly thing in front of our guests?"

Winston remained dramatically stoic as he answered, "Grace, you know I always wear my Captain's hat while sailing. How else are Anna and Joey to know that they are in capable hands?"

Joey imagined some guy finding a pilot's uniform at a thrift store and suddenly thinking he could fly an airliner. He shook the thought from his mind. Winston and Grace seemed perfectly comfortable on the constantly rocking craft. Without words, they began to pull ropes through pulleys as large sheets of fabric climbed the mast.

"Is everyone ready to cast off?" Winston asked with surprising authority. With absolutely zero experience, Joey and Anna looked for something to hold onto as Grace pulled loose the last rope holding them to the pier. The sail had been "in irons," flapping uselessly in the stiff breeze. With a quick adjustment of the mainsail, the sail popped into its rounded shape and the little vessel began to move forward as if some invisible force under the water was pulling it along. As they moved away from the marina toward open water, Winston again tightened the mainsail, causing the craft to heel over and accelerate. Anna clutched the railing with wide eyes and a nervous smile.

Winston seemed to be in his element. Of course, sailing would be a normal pastime of the upper class right along with polo or cricket. Unifying man, vessel and mother nature, it was if he was following some invisible trail that the winds were revealing to him.

"Coming about!" he shouted as the passengers ducked their heads. The mast swung across as the boat changed directions and began a new tack. It heeled to the opposite side as the invisible hand of God continued to push them along.

The motorboat containing the guards followed along about a quarter mile behind. They scanned the area, but the threat level was low for obvious reasons.

Chapter 99

May 27, 2012

Scullex, Taggart

Despite his best efforts to deceive, Chester could not convince the boat rental staff that he was experienced with anything that floated. Try as he may, he could not sufficiently answer any questions with enough terminology to satisfy their concerns. They offered the rental of a kayak, but he could see himself quickly capsizing in the low chop. Flustered and nursing a headache, he finally abandoned the ruse and was sulking down the peer when he noticed a pontoon boat idling against the buoys.

"Cliffs of Muldon Tours – Captain Alfred Jennings" was printed on the signs attached to its railings. Adorned with a variety of cameras, large hats and noses painted with suntan lotion, ten tourists waited for their guide/driver to board. In a moment of inspiration, Chester offered his best Taggish accent as he opened the low railing door and stepped aboard.

"Lovely day for a float. Is everyone ready to get underway?" he asked. Some looked dubiously at the large camera hung around his neck and his disheveled appearance, but they too were foreigners. Expectations can vary when visiting other countries. He understood enough to put the boat in gear and push the throttle forward when the ropes went tight, pulling the boat against the pier.

"Clumsy me!" he offered. "In my haste, I forgot to cast off the lines!" He struggled with the knots for a few moments until the boat drifted free. Once again pushing the throttle forward, the boat drifted and scraped against another boat moored just ahead. A few gasps and shouts of alarm were heard as he tried to pacify them.

"Bloody crosswinds. Welcome to the Taggish Channel!"

Once he was pointed in the right direction, he pushed the throttle all the way forward as the rental staff and a well-dressed tour boat captain pursued helplessly down the pier.

Chapter 100
May 27, 2012
Scullex, Taggart

Winston was feeling an immense sense of pride as he instructed his newest landlubbers in the art of sailing. Joey smiled as he watched Anna manning the helm and holding onto the mainsail. He was so grateful that she was his. His mind mentally photographed the moment.

The guards had a well-rehearsed and understood agreement for discretion. As much as could be allowed, they lingered in the distance and tried their best to remain only in the fringes of vision. Winston and Grace had long understood that their presence was an unfortunate yet necessary element of royal life.

"Oi! Some wanker is coming up on the port side," the guard shouted out to his shipmates. They languidly observed the pontoon boat pounding through the chop as it closed on the sailboat. The guards frowned with puzzlement as they noticed the passengers were fiercely holding onto the railings as the boat slammed through the waves. Hats flew off heads and a small, yellow camera fell over the side as passengers tried to steady themselves. The captain looked fixated on the sailboat ahead and looked suspiciously American. Little warning lights began going off in the minds of the guards.

"A little far out for a tour boat," one stated. Unconsciously, he performed a press check on his weapon to make sure a round was in the chamber. The safety remained on, but his thumb toyed with the lever. Without a PA system, they angled their boat to draw alongside the suspicious vessel.

Chester was determined to seize the moment and grab "the shot." He only needed one and he was almost within range. As far as he knew, the sailors were oblivious to his presence. He should have noticed the escort boat with the armed guards, but he was blinded by vengeance and dulled by fatigue. Only when they closed to within twenty feet and displayed their rifles did he realize his predicament.

His mind began to rapidly consider his options. Being so close to his objective after overcoming so many obstacles, he was not about to pull back on the throttle. He knew he couldn't outrun them, but he had two advantages. The first was that he had human shields. He knew the guards would never fire amongst the petrified passengers. Secondly, this was a rental.

Without contemplating the consequences, he yanked the wheel to the left, causing an elderly lady to fall across the deck onto the starboard side passengers. Shouts of anger and fear could be heard over the screaming outboard engine. The last thing the guards were expecting was to be rammed. Chester didn't want to sink them so much as disable them. Ducking down behind the console, he looked through the tiny windshield and aimed the front corner toward their engine.

With wide eyes and much shouting, the guards braced for impact as the larger aluminum barge struck their outboard motor. There were a sickening clank and the screeching of metal on metal as it broke off from its mount and fell into the green waters, its spinning propeller causing it to summersault on the surface before sinking. The guards continued shouting and raised their rifles, which caused the already terrified passengers to shriek and hit the deck. Chester felt victorious elation as he turned away from the stranded boat and continued to pursue his prey. He imagined that moments like this were what made the life of pirates so appealing.

Chapter 101
May 27, 2012
Scullex, Taggart

Winston noticed that Grace's tranquil expression suddenly displayed some concern. Something in their wake had caught her attention and he could see that she was reluctant to point it out because it would stifle the wonderful mood that had been constructed.

Winston turned and wrinkled his brow as he noticed the escort boat falling away and a peculiar pontoon boat now taking its place. He squinted at the guards, who were frantically making a signal with their arms above their heads. His heart froze. It was the Mayday signal. It was only to be used if a situation developed where they could no longer provide adequate protection. The signal was always part of the safety briefings, but no one really expected it to ever be needed.

"Everyone please get down in the hold. Hide your

faces," Winston tersely ordered. Anna and Joey thought it might be some type of strange Taggish humor until they saw Grace immediately obey. The concern on Winston's face served as further persuasion, so they both laid down like logs beside the duchess.

Winston explained to his horizontal crew. "Something is amiss. Our guards have fallen away and we are being pursued by a stranger." Winston thought as he surveyed his surroundings and adjusted the rudder. "Surely, it's not that same man from Salmon."

From their cramped position, Anna looked at Grace's anguished face and suddenly felt even more uneasy.

Joey decided to ask. "What guy from Salmon? Our Salmon?"

"His name is Chester Hannigan. He operates a tabloid in the States and has apparently set his sights on us. Intelligence believes he somehow gained knowledge of our holiday and the resulting calamity. We have done our best to suppress those unfortunate events as well as your identities, but he seems uncommonly determined."

"Our identities?" Anna asked with horror.

Winston's jaw was set as he swung the boom and selected another tack. The boat heeled over farther than it had all day. He shifted onto the starboard side and leaned his body backward over the water.

Grace picked up the explanation. "Being friends with us could ruin your lives. I could not rest until we properly thanked you for saving me, but we were not expecting to become so fond of you. It seems all our other acquaintances are just that. They are nothing more than social obligations and we feel that no one truly enjoys our company other than for what we can offer."

The small boat buffeted on the worsening waves as it picked up even more speed.

"What happens if he catches us?" Anna asked as the floor battered and bounced her around.

"Best case scenario? We all appear on the front page for a few days and then life goes back to normal," Grace answered.

"Worst case?"

"You can't go back to normal life. Everywhere you go, there are cameras and paparazzi. You have no privacy. You find people hiding in your bushes, stealing your personal items. And the rumors." Grace rolled her eyes at the thought.

"Don't worry. I think we might be able to shake them," Winston announced with firm resolve. His eyes darted between the top of the sail and the surface of the water around them.

By now, they could all hear the outboard motor approaching.

He began to tie a piece of rope around the tiller handle. "Hold on!" Winston shouted. With that, he yanked the mainsail from its cleat and swung the rudder hard to starboard. Slipping down onto the floor, the boat swung around 180 degrees and began picking up momentum in the other direction.

Winston pulled the boat cover from a hatch and motioned for everyone to cover up. The sound of the engine slowed and then quit entirely as the boats passed by at a close distance. A camera clicked about a dozen times, followed by a string of curse words. Complaints of tourists in various languages completed the exchange and increased in intensity.

It sounded as if mutiny were afoot.

Winston dared a peak from underneath the cover and could see multiple elderly people converging on the pontoon boat's console. He kept his hat down low but used the rope to adjust their course to pick up speed away from the troubled tour. He grinned at the others. "I think Chester has his hands full at the moment."

Chapter 102

May 27, 2012

Scullex, Taggart

When the authorities arrived, Chester had the nerve to attempt to blend in with the other passengers. Unfortunately for him, there were the witness statements of four angry guards and ten seasick tourists. Back at the marina, the two couples were quickly whisked away by a waiting Range Rover SUV. Back at the cottage, there was a static in the ambient mood. They sat around a table of uneaten sandwiches, each looking melancholy.

Anna spoke first. "This isn't going to work, is it?"

They met each other's eyes, but it seemed like no one knew how to respond. Then Joey spoke. "Not gonna work?" There was an edge to his voice, but it wasn't directed toward his friends. "I think I just went sailing in the Taggish Channel with the Prince of Taggart!"

"I'm a Duke, actually," Winston meekly responded.

"Whatever. I'm just saying this ain't nothin' to be upset about. If there's something I'm learning about life, it's that you can't always see setbacks as bad things. Did nobody else think that was super exciting?" He looked around at the others for understanding, but brows were furrowed in thought.

Grace spoke. "We couldn't bear the thought of ruining your lives."

"Ruining what lives? Runnin' the rat race? Trying to make ends meet? Stuck in Salmon?" Joey retorted.

"We rather liked Salmon," Winston said almost to himself.

"We like it too but that's not the point. This is the best thing that could have happened to us. Meeting you guys shook us up, got us out of a rut. We needed this."

"We needed you," Anna sweetly added.

The four looked at each other. There was a moment of pause before Winston confronted the group with a devilish grin. "So, is this worth it? Do we risk being discovered? Do you dare to be associated with the illustrious Winston and Grace?"

Joey turned to Anna. "Would you mind if people caught you out in town with these two yahoos?"

She smiled as she appreciated her husband's ability to simplify complicated situations. "We don't want it to end this way. We don't want to lose you."

Anna and Grace hugged as Winston and Joey locked hands with a manly clasp. Winston then asked, "So what exactly is a yahoo?”

Chapter 103

May 28, 2012

Morwell, Taggart

In a rare display of emotion, the Queen looked appalled. "What do you mean, 'a slight maritime dilemma?'"

Bancroft was once again walking the fine line of divided allegiance. His primary loyalties were to her majesty, but his fondness of Winston was impossible to deny. Upon attending the daily staff briefing, he knew he would have to choose his words carefully.

"It seems that the boat in which the guards were riding experienced the loss of a motor. They were temporarily stranded."

"Stranded? As in unable to provide adequate protection for their charge?"

"For only the briefest of moments. I assure you that Master Winston had complete control of the situation. He's quite the sailor, you know."

"Now, Bancroft. Please do not attempt to placate me by flattering my grandchildren."

I'm glad she doesn't know about the other boat! he thought with an inward sigh of relief.

Chapter 104

May 30, 2012

Morwell, Taggart

Normal criminal procedures were circumvented in the name of national security. Going through the court system would have required the incarceration of Chester Hannigan for quite some time, but it would also expose the perceived folly and failure of the Royal Guard. It was decided that he would be deported from the country and banned from re-entry. The three days that'd he'd spent in the detention cell would have to be considered sufficient justice.

Angry and embarrassed but not willing to admit defeat, Chester sat once again in the very last seat of a transatlantic flight that was now heading west. His mind was awash with various plots for revenge. He was too bullheaded to leave it alone. As soon as the plane touched down and he cleared customs, he opened his phone and sent a text.

Outgoing: SENDING PICS FOR THE PACKET. WAITING ON SILVER BULLET. HAVE YOU TESTED?

Incoming: TEST SUCCESSFUL. WAITING TO LOWER THE BLADE.

Chapter 105

June 1, 2012

Salmon, Idaho

Touching down in the place that was familiar to them came with both comfort and disappointment. After the "holiday" they had enjoyed, it was easy to understand the conflict. As the SUV dropped them off at their humble home, they hugged Peter goodbye. He had become a wonderful part of their lives. As the vehicle pulled out on the highway and disappeared, they wondered if they would ever see their friends again. The settling dust made them wonder if it had all been a dream.

Scott swung by that evening and dropped off the key Joey had given him.

"So, you guys went on a trip?" he asked.

"Yeah. We got out town for a few days."

Scott couldn't help but to be curious. Plus, it's polite to ask about vacations. "Go anywhere fun?"

"Taggart, actually. We hung out with the royal family, rode in their helicopter, went sailing in the Taggish Channel." Joey looked straight faced at Scott, who didn't know how to respond to something so absurd.

Joey let it linger for about ten seconds before he grinned and feigned a punch at Scott's mid-section. "I'm just messin' with you. Man, you're too easy."

Scott relaxed and laughed good-naturedly at what he perceived as a joke. He paused. "Well, everything was fine around here. I checked on the house and made sure the chickens had water."

"Thanks, Scott. I owe you."

"I'm glad to see you're doing better," Scott offered sincerely. "You are doing better, right?" he asked with raised eyebrows.

Joey smiled. "Yeah. We really are. I'm not sure if I owe that to you or someone else, but thank you."

Scott nodded but then continued. "But seriously, where'd you go?"

Chapter 106

June 10, 2012

Morwell, Taggart

It was Sunday night and they felt too exhausted to contemplate starting another hectic week in just a few hours. It had not taken long to be swept up in the whirlwind of responsibilities and obligations. They had been able to use Grace's rehabilitation as an excuse for only so long. The press was beginning to push and rumors were being published. An effort was made to show them publicly doing very normal tasks, including the entertainment of foreign dignitaries throughout the weekend. It was pure drudgery.

As Grace slipped off her high heels, she plopped onto the bed and slumped her shoulders. Winston plopped down beside her, almost perfectly mirroring her body language. Wearily, she rolled her head toward him and said, "I miss our friends. I miss the countryside." She then looked out into the distance. "I miss Idaho."

He contemplated her words before answering. "It's queer, isn't it? It's such a simple place and they are simple people, if we're being honest."

She looked at him as she tried to decipher his direction. "It's rather wonderful, really. I envy them."

She put her head on his shoulder as he continued thinking aloud. "Could you imagine us, living out in rural America, doing farmwork, eating fast food and driving pickup trucks?" The image wasn't entirely unpleasant.

They sat there, decompressing. "What would you do if we could go back there?" he asked.

She tilted her head as she imagined herself in Anna's shoes. "How would it be to leave the house whenever you pleased, no security escort, being able to slouch, not being perfect but completely comfortable?"

"How do you suppose you would handle the uncertainty?"

"I don't believe anyone can truly escape uncertainty. Our station provides a great deal of security, but it also comes with its share of perils." She asked with vacant eyes and a voice hollow of emotion, "Or have you forgotten our squirmish on the high seas?"

He laughed at her macabre humor and mispronunciation of the work skirmish. He knew she was tired.

"How do you suppose you would manage?" she softly asked. It felt nice to talk about such things.

"I suppose I had a very small taste of it in the air

force. It was nice to be 'one of the guys' to some degree."

"A very small degree" she flatly added. He looked at her. "Come now, Winston. You know how very proud I am of your service, but even then you were heavily monitored. Your normal is nowhere near the normal of others. It can't be."

The truth of her words stung just a bit. He, too, now searched some distant realm of thought for some enlightenment. He thought of Grace's many smiles as they had galivanted to obscure locations and the time they had spent with Joey and Anna. Yes, they were friends, but they also represented something. They were a version of themselves if their fates had been different. He was born into royalty. Grace, in a unique twist, seemed destined for it. How could another naturally look and act so much like a princess?

They sat there, exhausted and introspective. Although neither spoke it aloud, they were both wondering what it would be like to truly be normal. How would it be to spit in public, wear sweatpants, get in a fist fight, skip the makeup? At the moment, those things seemed like more fantasy, much the way Taggart had seemed to Anna and Joey.

Chapter 107
June 11, 2012
Morwell, Taggart

In all honesty, Olivia "the bloodhound" had enjoyed the last two weeks of high alert. In her analytical, compartmented life, the recent seriousness of work had been a nice break from the tedium. They had all come together as a unit to extinguish any hint of intrusion or libel. The in-house briefings on the arrest of the American had been the subject of much debate and conversation. Most had felt that the right course of action had been taken, whereas a few more militant opinions felt that "permanent removal" was justified. If only James Bond really existed.

The next day would be a return to the usual. They were lowering their threat level and resuming normal shifts. Olivia felt a tinge of melancholy. She had enjoyed the feeling of serving a higher purpose.

Chapter 108

June 12, 2012

Chicago, Illinois

The trail had gone cold but the anger in his heart had not. Chester looked at every photograph he had collected so far but there just wasn't anything solid. The back sides of bodies, questionable profiles, grainy resolution – there was nothing here worth posting. Tempting as it may be to go with his own observations, he knew that would be media suicide without any photos to back it up. He slammed his fist on the desk thinking of how close he'd been. There were other potential stories that offered plenty of scandal, but they were little fish in comparison. He wanted the one that got away.

Although he had his contacts on high alert, everything was quiet. He was a patient hunter, but it felt like his winter had come and his prey had gone into hibernation.

Chapter 109

June 18, 2012

Salmon, Idaho

The day had been long and supper had been good. Joey and Anna sat on the couch watching a television show about a boss and employee who accidentally got married at a work conference in Vegas. It was shallow and predictable but a nice way to unwind before bed. The phone on the wall rang, which was unusual for this time of night. He looked at her to see if she was expecting to hear from anyone. She shrugged, indicating that she was not. She got up and picked up the receiver.

"Hello?" Her eyes lit up. "Grace! How are you doing? We've missed you."

Joey stood up and listened to one side of the conversation.

"We have...Yes...We did...Yes...Of course!...How about you?...Wow!...I can't imagine."

Joey felt impatient. *What were they talking about? How is Winston? Are we gonna see them again?* He knew his thoughts were childish, but he didn't care.

The call continued. "Sure...I guess. OK. OK...OoooooK?...I'm not sure...please...Ok."

Joey wanted to snatch the phone away and demand to speak to Winston. *What is going on here? Why do I feel like this?* He crossed his arms impatiently as she turned away.

"I'm not sure...What would they even look like...A beard?...No way...No way!...NO WAY!!!...Ok...Let me know...We'll talk soon."

She casually hung up the phone and walked back to the couch, where she sat down and picked up the remote. He stood there staring at her with his mouth open. When she continued to play games by absentmindedly changing the channels, he called her name.

"Anna?"

"Hmmm?"

"Are you gonna tell me what that was all about?"

"Oh. Wrong number."

He leapt across the room and landed on his knees on the couch. He grabbed her by the waist and tickled her. "You will tell me or else," he threatened in a menacing tone. She was squirming and cackling. She loved him. "Tell me," he repeated in a deeper tone as he intensified the tickling.

"OK, OK," she said with her hands up as she caught

her breath. He waited for her until she looked him in the eyes and then declared, "The Taggish are coming! The Taggish are coming!" It earned her another round of tickling.

Chapter 110

July 1, 2012

Morwell, Taggart

Sergeant Bosworth was at a loss. His two most trusted corporals stood at attention, eyes locked on some spot on the wall. He paced back and forth as he searched the floor for some explanation. Finally, he stopped to address them.

"How could this have happened? How could YOU have let this happen?"

The men knew that this wasn't directly their fault, although it could easily be hung around their necks. Despite their loyalty to the crown, each man's mind began to assign blame to others and fabricate excuses. Their job title was to guard and not babysit. Winston and Grace were adults. Did they have the right to keep them locked in their rooms? Take away their car keys? Instate a curfew?

The sergeant continued.

"I want every available resource on this now! Wait. Belay that. Don't let it leave this room. Tell no one." The sergeant's ambivalence indicated how troubled he was by this. The Idaho incident had been a close call and the little stunt on the English Channel should have never happened. Now this? For the first time in his career, he felt his nerves starting to fray.

He paced some more before deciding on a course of action. "You two. Change into civilian clothing and track them. Use secure channels and carry false documents. Develop a cover story and deny everything else until instructed otherwise. Is that clear?"

"Yes, Sergeant!" they answered in unison.

"Dismissed," he said coolly before collapsing at his desk and taking some headache medicine.

Chapter 111

July 1, 2012

Morwell, Taggart

That same morning, two planes took off from Hedgerow within fifteen minutes of each other. Each was transporting an American tourist back to some obscure town in the United States after short layovers in Atlanta and New York, respectively. The earlier plane welcomed aboard a fairly plump young lady with shoulder length bleached blonde hair. She wore a loose jogging suit with "JUICY" in large letters across the front. Oversized sunglasses obscured a face that had way too much makeup and jewelry. She smacked gum and seemed to make it a point to be obnoxious and annoying. People gave her a width berth and avoided eye contact.

A young man boarded the later plane but looked entirely out of place with the working-class commuters and traveling families. He was slender except for his stomach. He wore a cowboy hat and sported a dark beard that made him look like a tall Chuck Norris. His boots and faded jeans were topped by an untucked t-shirt that said "Cheyenne Frontier Days, 2011." It had the silhouette of a bull rider on the back. He had a canvas rucksack over his shoulder that made him look like he'd spent last night on the trail. Later than day, both flights eventually terminated in Boise, where a young couple was waiting in the terminal with a cardboard sign that simply said "Dukes." It was a clever play on words.

Chapter 112

July 1, 2012

Morwell, Taggart

Corporals Robinson and Bailey, now dressed in regular clothes, showed their credentials and entered the private living quarters of Winston and Grace. Opening the door, everything appeared neat and orderly. There was no sign of struggle. Nothing appeared to be missing. However, there was a solitary envelope on the bed addressed to "The Royal Guard." The two men exchanged glances then agreed that they were the intended audience. Robinson took up the envelope and was about to open it when he observed some writing along the back edge where it was sealed:

Please wait three days before opening. We are safe and will explain our absence then. W & G

The men looked at each other before Bailey spoke. "The Sergeant is not going to like this."

Chapter 113

July 1, 2012

Chicago, Illinois

Depressive states can strike without warning. Chester slept in and finally awoke with a strange void in his inner spirit. He just wasn't feeling it today. He searched within himself for that anger, that need for revenge, that hatred of the royal family but it just wasn't there. He laid in bed for a while and realized with a fair amount of surprise that he really didn't have to do anything. Eventually, he got out of bed and lumbered toward the kitchen where the coffee maker soon provided him with a hot cup of brew. He sat at the counter in his apartment and, for some reason, became very curious about his neighborhood. After a quick mental discussion with himself, he put on some athletic clothes and went outside.

After only a block, he discovered a cafe on the corner that he had driven past hundreds of times but never noticed. Shrugging, he pulled open the door and went inside. Minutes later, he continued his walk with a fresh pastry and a latte. *Why not? I should enjoy not being in some dungeon in Morwell.* The thought made him laugh at himself: the horrible flight, the shocking experience at the cottage, ramming a boat full of royal guards. He shook his head. *What on earth was I thinking?* Age was happening in his body and apparently now in his mind as well. Maybe his hunting days were over. Maybe he should just live and let live. The people he had exposed were probably not going to change. Sure, he'd made a quick buck and shook things up, but the satisfaction was always short lived.

He turned into a small park and found a bench overlooking a duck pond. Eating his pastry, he began to consider the future and how he could redirect his talents and abilities. With no pressing plans, he allowed his mind to drift to areas previously unexplored. Sitting there with his head cocked slightly to the side for almost an hour, he finally had a revelation.

I'm starting a non-profit.

Its purpose would be for underprivileged kids who wanted to get into journalism. He would give classes on photography, creative writing, marketing, interviewing techniques. He'd even thought of a name: Extra! Extra! News for a New Generation.

Walking back to his apartment, he felt like a new man. He even felt benevolent. It was time to turn a corner, turn over a new leaf. He would erase and destroy all of his old files and make an appointment with his attorney to get the paperwork started.

Unlocking the door, he went inside of his apartment and tossed his keys on the counter, where they slid to a stop next to a blinking cell phone. Out of habit, he looked at it and saw an unread text from his contact.

Incoming: TROUBLE AT THE PALACE. WINSTON AND GRACE RUMORED TO BE MISSING.

Chester looked up from the phone and his eyes narrowed. And just like that, the old him was back.

Chapter 114

July 1, 2024

Boise, Idaho

The superficially dressed couple should have won the Oscar for their acting. Blending in with the crowd, they walked their own path, didn't say "excuse me" and acted like they owned the airport. Ironically, it's how you would expect royalty to act.

Joey and Anna hugged the bleached blonde and the cowboy. Stepping back, they looked at their friends, shook their heads and laughed. Anna had a great idea and asked a stranger to take a photo of them and their friends who'd just returned from an overseas vacation. The four threw their arms around each other and struck silly poses while making funny faces. The kind stranger took several shots and smiled politely before returning the camera and walking away.

In her normal (but quiet) voice, Grace leaned in to speak with Anna. "This is amazing! They haven't a clue as to who we are." She was looking around the terminal as if she had just been released from prison and was seeing the world for the first time.

Winston was still in character but had now inserted a toothpick into his mouth and was standing with his thumb tucked into his belt and one hip cocked to the side. Throw in a lit cigarette and lasso and he'd be the new Marlboro Man.

"You guys are crazy," Joey said with a smile. "I can't believe you're doing this, but we're glad you are."

Grace switched over to a forced but fairly believable American accent as they began to walk toward the parking deck.

"We had to. It's hard to explain but, if we didn't, I don't think we could go on."

"We know this is just a short break, but we need this, just like you needed Scullex," Winston contributed.

"Well, we are gonna' take the I of Idaho, as my dad used to say."

They loaded their bags into the minivan and the royal couple had to remind themselves that no one was there to open their doors. Jumping in, they buckled up as Joey rolled down the windows. Joey let out a loud "YeeeeHA!" as they pulled out onto the highway.

Winston looked playfully at Grace right before they belted out their own weird, Taggish/American version.

"Yiieee-HO!"

Chapter 115

July 1, 2012

Morwell, Taggart

I mpetuous, reckless, thoughtless, rash, foolhardy," she muttered scornfully to herself. The only thing more impressive than her vocabulary was her current state of anger. The Queen was not given to strong emotion or outburst, but this was an entirely new and shocking predicament.

Bancroft dutifully stood by and exercised his usual self-discipline by not reacting in the slightest. He'd seen her majesty's wings ruffled on rare instances but this was, by far, her most expressive fit.

"One does not simply disappear," she said aloud. She turned to Bancroft. "Did you know about this?"

"No, Your Majesty. I was only made aware of this at this morning's security briefing."

The Queen was upset and her human nature needed someone to blame. "Where did I go wrong? When did I fail them?" She put a hand to her mouth to hide the quivering of her bottom lip.

Bancroft could see both sides to this. Yes, it was unheard of and, frankly, rude. Winston and Grace knew quite well that everyone would be worried sick. On the other hand, what choice did they have? Doesn't every young couple deserve to be wild and free to some degree?

The Queen turned to her trusted butler of so many years. Her eyes were filled with loss and fear. She looked up at him, desperately seeking some reassurance or comfort.

"Oh, Bancroft." With that, she took a step toward him and placed her head against his chest. Violating every rule of etiquette that his position required, he put his arm around her and placed his hand on her back. They remained like this for as long as she needed.

Chapter 116

July 1, 2012

Lowman, Idaho

Almost two hours into their drive, Joey slowed the minivan and pulled off of the curvy, mountainous highway into a wooded campground. Each couple changed into their swimsuits and put on water shoes before he led them down a set of stairs toward an amazingly scenic river flowing through the bottom of a deep gorge. Water and steam poured out of algae covered rocks near the boulder strewn shore where pools had been constructed from stacks of flat rocks. Joey eased into the water, followed by Anna and eventually Winston and Grace.

"And just anyone can use these?" Grace asked.

"Well, yeah. It's kinda hard to block off nature, although folks try."

The water was really too hot to touch near its source, but it was just right after running across the rocks and mixing with the water of the pools. They settled in and looked up at the robin egg blue sky as wispy clouds lazily floated past.

"I could stay here forever," Winston said aloud.

"You might wanna' hydrate, if you do." Joey reached into his nearby backpack and tossed Winston a bottle of water. "The high mineral content is good for you, but you need to drink."

The cool water running down his throat felt like nectar. "It's amazing how the right circumstances can make the banal feel incredible."

Joey looked concerned as he asked, "Winston? You been having problems with your banal?"

Winston and Grace exchanged puzzled glances before bursting out in laughter.

Joey and Anna remained confused.

Chapter 117

July 1, 2012

Middle America

Old habits die hard. Apparently, former tabloid hounds do too. Chester wasn't in the last row of the plane this time, but the young boy behind him kicked his seat back approximately once every three seconds. He would have usually stood and glared at the perpetrator (and his mother) but today, he just sat there and allowed his fury to brew. He was bent on getting "the shot." That old feeling in his gut was stronger than ever and he knew that the royal couple had gone back to Idaho for some strange reason. Whatever secret Salmon was hiding, he was going to find out. This wasn't Taggart. He had the home field advantage and he had the sneaky suspicion that there would be no royal guards to contend with this time. Yes, this would be his triumph. He would seize a large share of the European market and, with Spyder's help, those toads in Morwell wouldn't be able to do a single thing about it. He leaned back in his seat as a sinister, crooked smile stretched across his face. Kick - Kick - Kick.

Chapter 118

July 1, 2012

Somewhere Across the Atlantic

Without compromising their allegiance, they had reported to the Sergeant but omitted their discovery of the letter. After finding a hair dye container in the wastebasket, they suggested that Winston and Grace may have returned to Idaho to visit their new friends. Now, Corporals Robinson and Bailey were flying west with orders to locate and observe the royal couple without detection.

Chapter 119

July 1, 2012

Salmon, Idaho

After dropping off their bags, they once again loaded up into the minivan and were driving to a surprise event that Joey called "A real American experience."

Winston asked, "How is it that you drive a minivan even though you have no children? I had assumed that someone like you would be driving a vehicle equipped with large tires and a loud exhaust pipe."

Joey shrank at the slightly demeaning question. "I lost it."

Winston neglected to notice Joey's obvious tone and body language, which should have warned him that it was a sensitive subject. "Lost it? Oh dear! I've lost lots of things in my life but never an entire vehicle!" He was grinning and expecting a lighthearted response from his friends.

Anna turned around and answered, "What he means is that the bank repossessed it. We couldn't make the payments anymore."

Winston's grin faded into gloom as he realized his gaffe. Wanting to somehow help and make the situation better, he offered, "Well, Grace and I would be glad to purchase a new truck." Grace nodded approvingly but Joey held up his hand.

"Thanks, Winston. I know your heart and I appreciate it, but this is a hole I need to dig myself out of. It's an honor thing."

Winston's tone was instantly more even and compassionate. "I suppose your lives and their associated struggles are quite foreign to us. So this minivan is your only means of transportation and it is not by choice?"

Anna answered, "My folks let us borrow it until we can get back on our feet. I've been selling eggs and picking up extra shifts at the daycare. Joey is working at a friend's ranch on the weekends."

Winston connected the dots. He stated his understanding slowly. "And you took off this weekend to spend time with us. You've sacrificed your much needed extra income for our sake."

Joey squinched his mouth as he searched for a way to restore the joyful mood. "Look. I appreciate your concern, and I know you'd step in in a heartbeat if I asked. But I'm learning that things work out if you do the right thing. They just do. We're gonna be just fine. I'm not worried about it. Anna's not worried about it. And I don't want you two to be worried about it. Being here with you, right now, is the most important thing in our lives. And we intend to make the most of it."

Thankfully, their destination was coming up on the right as Joey slowed down to turn. The strange glow of bright lights mingled with dust filled the sky as the unmistakable scent of horse hooey and straw entered the vehicle. As they parked in the dirt lot besides hundreds of other vehicles, Joey turned around and grinned as he announced, "Welcome to the rodeo."

Chapter 120

July 1, 2012

Salmon, Idaho

It had been another harrowing five-hour drive, but Chester had managed to avoid careening down any chasms or canyons. When he passed the Salmon City Limits sign, he brought the rented Kia Soul down from 20 over to 10 under the speed limit. He was on the prowl. His gut confirmed that he was not only on the right trail this time, but he was close. Very close. He drove past City Hall and slowed even more as he passed by the Sip-N-Shake.

"Show yourselves," he almost hissed to himself.

That's when he noticed the flyer taped to a telephone pole. **Salmon Stampede, June 29th - July 1st.**

"Jackpot!" he shouted as he accelerated to the edge of town and into the dusty parking area. Grabbing his camera, he pledged himself to break any law and violate any expectation of privacy for the sake of the getting "the shot."

Chapter 121

July 1, 2012

Salmon, Idaho

Nobody batted an eye at the two couples decked out in cowboy boots, jeans and t-shirts. Winston blended in especially well with the hat and toothpick. Grace thought it was rather silly (but admittedly liked the way he looked). Corn dogs and funnel cakes were purchased as they made their way to the bleachers. Everything smelled like livestock and clouds of dust swirled in the banks of flood lights. Country music blared through PA speakers in between announcements from the rodeo emcee.

From angry broncos to barrel racing to sad faced clowns, Winston and Grace loved the spectacle. Several times they gasped or laughed, making sure to sound as unrefined and American as possible. From moment to moment, it was almost possible to forget who they were. After complete rides or crazy moments, the guys would high five and make commentary. The girls were catching up on life while halfway watching the show.

The evening reached its halftime when the emcee announced in a booming, goading voice, "Who in our crowd is ready to ride the beast?" The crowd roared back as some fairly intoxicated men stood and pointed to themselves with both hands. A few ladies stood and tugged at their date's arm, who shyly stayed seated.

"How 'bout it, Tex?" Joey asked Winston.

"Is this a real thing? They actually allow members of the audience to ride the bulls?"

"Well, it's not one of the really mean bulls but, yeah, they do. The usually won't let you ride if you've been drinking a bunch."

"Have you done it?"

"Yeah, when I was younger." Joey smiled at the memory.

The girls piped in. "We want to see it! Yeah, show us what you got!"

The guys looked at each other and knew that this moment required a decision. The smart move was to demur and watch some other fool get thrown through the air and knocked silly. However, real men respond to a challenge, especially when it's made by pretty girls. Both of their expressions instantly became serious and excessively macho. Joey shrugged his consent and Winston was obligated to do the same. Trying to hide any doubts or fears, they spoke hesitantly as they stood and excused themselves.

"Well, uh, we should, um, probably go get in line," Joey stammered.

"This will be one for the scrapbooks," Winston offered.

Chapter 122

July 1, 2012

Salmon, Idaho

Chester's Press Pass could have fooled anybody. He'd used it countless times to go backstage at various events or celebrity appearances. Wearing the lanyard around his neck, he took random photographs and played the part of an everyday reporter.

Alright, I know you're here. Where are you? he thought as he panned the camera across the crowd. He didn't expect to find them in a section cordoned off with velvet ropes and security guards. No. If his hunch was correct, they would be in disguise. From what he had gathered, their disappearance was unscheduled and unauthorized. Surely, they would be smart enough to keep a low profile and blend in.

"Next up is Joey, the tornado!" the PA speaker boomed. Another fan was adjusting his grip on the rope tied around the bull's torso. To reduce the risk of injury, he wore a helmet with a faceguard and thick gloves.

"Ready? Let's ride!" the announcer shouted. The gate swung open and the bull did what it was supposed to. Kicking its back legs high in the air, the beast did its best to eject its passenger. After three bucks, it accomplished its mission. The rider lost his grip and flew over the animal's head where he landed and tumbled in the thick sawdust. A crew of clowns rushed in to release the strap and distract the bull.

Chester snapped another random picture of the rider as other clowns hoisted him over the wall and helped him remove his helmet. As the crowd cheered for him, he turned and waved at two particular girls up in the stands who were shouting their approval with fists held high. One blew a kiss toward the wannabe cowboy.

"Next up, we got Billy Bronco!" Another young man gingerly made his way onto the large bull. He didn't seem as comfortable as the previous rider. Although Chester couldn't care less about the event, he felt like he could sacrifice a few seconds of vigilance for a quick laugh. Out of habit, he turned his camera toward the pin and began to fire as the gate swung open.

Even through the facemask, the guy's wide eyes told the whole story. He was petrified, elated, panicked and having the time of his life.

"Look at him go!" the announcer bellowed. As the seconds ticked by, the crowd stood as the crescendoing shouts filled the arena.

"He may go all the way, folks!" The bull seemed infuriated at the thought of being conquered and spun around as he furiously kicked the air. And yet, the rider remained. Chester even found himself rooting for the brave stranger.

"Come on. Hang in there!" he absentmindedly uttered.

The emcee shouted "He's done it!" as a buzzer sounded. It was time for the rider to bail but apparently, he didn't know how. The bull intensified its dislike of the passenger as clowns rushed in to help. Nine seconds, ten seconds. The emcee began to shout.

"Let go! Jump!!!"

Just as the young man was able to release his grip, the bull gave one last fantastic, vengeful kick. The rider's arms windmilled as he sailed through the air. The helmet flew off as he completed an unintended flip and rolled head over heels. The crowd gasped audibly as a brief moment of chaos ensued. As Chester continued depressing the shutter button, a faint recognition began forming in his mind. The unmasked rider sat up and tried to get his bearings as the clowns did their work nearby. He had a beard and was dressed like every other male in the place, but there was something about his profile. The nose. The eyes. The wispy light-colored hair. He kept the shutter button down and looked over the camera at the two young ladies he'd noticed earlier. The blonde one had her hands to her mouth, her eyes conveying horror.

Could it? Is that? Chester silently asked himself. Turning the camera like a well-trained sniper, he said, "Gotcha," and held the shutter button down. The camera captured the shots like cards being shuffled. *Tat-tat-tat-tat-tat-tat-tat.* Back and forth, zooming out, zooming in, he must have taken a hundred frames.

Grace had been the target of paparazzi long enough to develop a sixth sense for when she was being photographed. Instantly, she noticed the long barrel camera that alternated between her and Winston. Her face revealed her shock at being discovered. She grabbed Anna's forearm, which surprised her already alarmed friend.

"He's found us," she desperately stated as she ducked her head and tried to cover her face. "No, no, no! This is not happening." Grace moved down the steps, her head turned away. Anna stood and followed, although she was obviously confused.

As Winston was pulled onto the wall, he realized that he was no longer wearing either helmet or cowboy hat. Panic covered his face as he looked for Grace and saw her moving quickly toward the parking lot. He instinctively scanned the audience and immediately saw the photographer, who was now pointing the camera directly at him.

Dread and anger filled his gut. Try as he may, he would never be able to free Grace from the crystal prison in which she now resided. Their initial trip to Idaho, their holiday in the countryside, the rodeo – they were all tainted by a destiny that was determined to prevent them from any sense of normalcy.

He had another choice, which had to be made right now. The prudent action was to run after Grace, secure her, make a phone call and be whisked away to a safe place where "the team" would do their best to suppress this most recent exposure. Unfortunately for Chester, Winston took the effect this would have on Grace personally.

The photos from Chester's camera would show a very determined (and bearded) Winston closing in. The face would deteriorate from anger into rage as his right hand balled into a fist. The face would fill up the frame as the fist passed by quickly to the left. The last frames would be of the night sky and then one showing the littered floor of the stands.

Joey had the minivan cranked and was pulling away as he asked, "Is everybody OK? Winston, who was that?"

Winston was red faced and trying to control his breathing. He had his arm around Grace, who was now crying and had her face buried in his chest. Anna looked worried.

They accelerated up the highway in silence. Several moments passed before Winston spoke to Grace. "It's over. We must call them."

Joey butted in. "Call who? Tell us what's going on so we can help."

"Someone identified us at the rodeo. He was clearly taking photos of Grace and me." He paused. "It's him."

Grace looked horrified as Winston continued. "It's Chester Hannigan. He's the one who caught wind of our rafting incident, sabotaged our Scullex holiday and has apparently now tracked us down to the rodeo." With his usual diplomacy, he looked out at the passing silhouette of the Idaho mountains before stating, "One must admire his tenacity and determination."

Anna felt sick. She cared for Grace and couldn't stand to see her like this. Joey fumed inside over not being able to do more to make this situation better, to somehow fix it. The minivan turned down the familiar dirt driveway and parked around back this time. They entered through the back door and closed all the curtains. This night lacked the jovial mood of their last sleepover.

Chapter 123

July 1, 2012

Unknown Location

The hour was ridiculously late but Spdyer didn't care. In the world of ones and zeroes, the cycle of night and day was irrelevant. The text appeared on the phone sitting near the computer terminal.

Incoming: CHECK THE FILE. PACKAGE DOWNLOADING.

Outgoing: PULL THE TRIGGER?

Incoming: FIRE AWAY.

Chapter 124

July 2, 2012

Morwell, Taggart

Olivia swiped her magnetic credential and accessed the secure facility the way she'd done for the past six years. Setting down her coffee, she turned on the monitor and entered her username and password. Slightly distracted by personal thoughts, she didn't immediately notice that her home screen now looked different. Instead of the beach scene that had been her recent background, there was now a Jolly Roger skull and crossbones.

Frowning, she tapped the keyboard and jiggled the mouse with no effect. She tapped Control-Alt-Delete, but it remained unresponsive. Her puzzlement became horror as the cursor began to move on its own. It opened files in the C: drive and began to transfer. Her heart froze as her wide eyes watched in horror.

"SECURITY BREACH!!!" she yelled at the top of her

lungs.

Chapter 125

July 2, 2012

Salmon, Idaho

Thanks to the Sergeant's forethought, Corporals Robinson and Bailey were already in the area when the phone call was made. They arrived at the Woodfords and secured the perimeter before reporting their status. Arrangements were made as Winston and Grace sat on the couch like grounded teenagers. They really had no say-so in the matter. They had taken a chance in disguising themselves and coming here, but it had bitten them.

Winston was cursing himself for his stupidity. He had apologized to Grace for the dozenth time. She had a weary, distant expression on her face. He had only wanted to surprise her; give her a much-needed break from the hustle and bustle of their daily lives. The way he'd seen her laugh and smile over the last few weeks had made him feel entirely successful. He also thought of the heartache of almost losing her, the repeated hops across the pond, the terror (and the thrill) of almost being caught multiple times. It had been a whirlwind that had become a tornado which had left a path of wreckage behind itself.

"Sir, Ma'am, the plane is ready. We should depart," Robinson said.

The two couples looked at each other and wondered what this all had been. The emotions had been so strong. The friendship had felt so genuine. The mutual relief and comfort that each offered to the other was undeniable. But it was all over now. Grace was the first to speak.

"We shall miss you." Her words were caught in her throat. "However, it does not seem that life is going to allow this." She motioned with her hand, which seemed to capture more than just the people sitting in this shabby living room. Her eyes dropped as her bottom lip began to quiver.

Anna wanted to rush to her side and put an arm around her, but it felt like something was now in the way. The invisible wall that invariably separates the famous from the obscure had slammed down hard. It now seemed permanent.

Joey and Winston stood, faced each other and shook hands in a very professional manner. Each man tried to speak, but a simple head nod was all they could manage. Robinson opened the door, which the royal couple walked through before plodding down the walkway and entering the open door of the SUV. Neither looked back as the door was closed.

Chapter 126

July 2, 2012

Salmon, Idaho

Mondays were typically busy for Scott. He was leaving his first appointment at the Henerson farm and was getting in his truck when his phone indicated an incoming text.

What now, Jacob? he thought with irritation. He never expected anything good from his brother.

Incoming: SALMON IS ON THE MAP! DIDN'T KNOW YOU RUBBED ELBOWS WITH ROYALTY. WOULD YOU CARE FOR A SPOT OF TEA?

Scott had no idea what his brother was talking about but dutifully clicked the attached link that appeared.

The screen filled with the Exposed-HD logo as heavy metal music began to play.

"Exposed-HD has been the first to bring you the hottest news from the world's most famous celebrities and their scandals." The voice was rough and dramatic like a wrestling announcer. "Buckle up because Exposed-HD is about to release an exclusive report that will knock your socks off!"

Scott frowned but continued to watch.

"The royal family lives in their own personal fairytale. Money, power, fame: they've had it for centuries. That money and power have guaranteed their secrecy but it couldn't save them from Exposed HD-D-D-d-d-d." The voice lowered in tone and echoed.

Images of Winston and Grace standing together and smiling filled the screen. They were well-dressed, on their best behavior and obviously in Morwell.

"Unless you've been living under a rock, you know these guys as The Duke and Duchess of Ulbridge. But did you know that Winston and Grace have been living double lives?" The heavy metal music continued to fill in the background. Photos of Joey and Anna appeared on the screen. There was another shot of their simple home with the dirt driveway. The next showed a short section of crime scene tape near a boat launch.

Scott was not expecting to see his hometown and especially not his friends.

"Who are these secret soulmates? Who's been spending the night with who? Humbington Palace is on fire with rumors of dissatisfied spouses and love affairs in the wild west."

Scott's stomach sank at the implications. He wanted to look away but, like a train wreck, he just couldn't.

"They say that near-death experiences form close bonds. What have they been hiding? Is a royal divorce on the horizon? Has Winston gone mad with jealousy?"

The next series of photos showed an angry Winston coming in close and obviously punching someone. The next photos showed Grace covering her face, running down the steps and out of the arena. The last photo showed Winston sitting in the dust with a bewildered look on his face. He looked confused and possibly drunk. The dusty outfit did little to defend his reputation.

"Winston and Grace, you've been exposed, HD Style-style-style-style."

The heavy metal music faded as the image slowly blurred into wavy lines. If the video was intended to cast the royal couple in a poor light, it had done an excellent job.

Chapter 127

July 2, 2012

Morwell, Taggart

I t had been a drastic but necessary decision. The axes mounted near the computer terminals had remained unused and curiously out of place, until now. With no way to regain control of the network and megabytes of files being transferred by the second, the director gave the command. Reluctantly but quickly, the analysts took the tools from their mounts and began the grisly task of smashing hard drives and severing cables. It took less than a minute, but the once well-organized computer lab was now a debris field of plastic, metal, silicon and glass.

Breathing heavily, Olivia held her ax and stared at the wreckage that used to be a haven of order and predictability. Her world had been violated. In spite of this, she felt grave concern for the royal family. She felt that she had let them down, which was almost the equivalent of treason in her mind. It caused her to think of a disgraced Samurai warrior who was compelled to commit hara-kiri. She shook the grisly thought from her mind. Everyone in the unit was reeling from a strong sense of defeat and helplessness. Where could they turn to for help? They had been the tip of the electronic spear that was now broken.

Chapter 128

July 2, 2012

Chicago, Illinois

He took the steak and held it against his swollen eye as he clicked "Play Again." For the twentieth time, he watched the clip that had just been released in the United States and in most European markets. After it ended, he clicked to another window and looked at the views. Their count was climbing faster than his eye could register. Despite his physical appearance, he felt like a champion. He leaned back in his leather chair and considered the resources of the royal family. Despite their money, military power and electronic security, he had won.

Chester versus the world, he thought.

The slightest twinge of sadness crept into the edges of his thought.

What now? Who is a bigger target than the royal family? Have I just climbed my Everest?

It was a foolish thought, which he dissolved by looking once more at the skyrocketing view counter.

Chapter 129
July 2, 2012
Salmon, Idaho

Joey and Anna didn't speak much. They felt the way a child does when their balloon flies away. As it recedes upward into the sky, you realize that you will never see it again. Joey made himself a sandwich and opened the door to head to work when he was met by a small army of photographers. Surprised by the strangers in his front yard, he ran back inside and shut the door.

"Anna! We're surrounded!"

She peeked through the curtains as her eyes widened. She remembered Grace's words describing the best and worst-case scenarios of falling into the press's crosshairs. Their moods went from bad to worse. Joey set down his lunch bag and looked at his wife. They stared at each other for a moment, knowing exactly what the other was thinking and not finding any words to make it right.

Chapter 130

July 2, 2012

Morwell, Taggart

Winston and Grace looked like school children waiting in the principal's office. They sat side by side on the small plush couch, looking at their shoes and not saying a word. Their heads jerked up in attention as the door opened. They quickly stood as Bancroft entered, followed by the Queen and Sergeant Bosworth. Everyone wore somber expressions.

The Queen walked directly in front of the young couple (who had assumed the demeanor of eight-year-olds) and simply stood there looking at them. Grace forced a slight smile, but Winston could not hold the Queen's gaze. He looked down with full realization that his actions had cost their family and their country an enormous amount of money, resources and anguish.

As the standoff continued, everyone wondered who would be first to speak. As decorum required, the Queen broke the ice.

"What do you have to say for yourselves?" Her inquiry was simple, devoid of malice but demanded a response.

Grace curtseyed and was about to speak when Winston held up his hand.

"It is entirely my fault. I wanted to surprise Gracelyn for our anniversary and, lamentably, everything began to unravel."

The Queen continued to stare into his face, which prodded him to expound. "While touring rural Idaho, I arranged for us to go whitewater rafting. Gracelyn fell overboard and..." his voice faltered with emotion, "I thought we had lost her."

She continued to listen patiently. He continued. "Fortunately, there was a man who was spending his holiday in the woods. He was able to rescue Gracelyn and carry her to safety. It was quite an exploit of bravery and resilience."

The Queen seemed sincerely surprised by this news. With eyebrows raised, she asked, "What have we done to recognize this man's selfless behavior? Has he been recognized?"

Grace chanced a quick glance at Winston to see how he would handle this.

"Well, he and his wife were given a tour of Scullex. They were hosted at the family's cottage," he said brightly.

The Queen seemed to see through this. "Ah, yes. The

nautical nonsense I was appraised of. How delightful."

Winston lowered his head again.

"So, what on earth transpired so that the two of you were photographed at a livestock auction dressed as common folk?" Although she had a reputation for extreme temperance, the question was laden with guilt inducing accusation.

"It was a rodeo," Winston offered lamely. "I was caught up in the moment."

"And do I understand correctly that this entire escapade was done without prior authorization? Thankfully, the Sergeant discovered your absence and initiated a brilliant plan of contingency."

Sergeant Bosworth bowed ever so slightly in acknowledgement.

"You have recklessly endangered the life of our beloved Gracelyn and the reputation of our family three times now. Both have been injured by your actions, and it has reached a point that I must intervene."

Winston and Grace braced themselves for their sentencing.

"All family assets are off limits until further notice. You will be provided local transportation for official use only. You will remain within the confines of the palace where monitoring by the royal guard will be heightened."

The young couple, now thirty years of age, was processing the conditions of their punishment. It sounded as if they were, in fact, being grounded.

Perhaps Winston could have taken this opportunity to defy the Queen, declare his independence as an adult, grab Grace's hand and storm out of the room. However, life was not that simple, especially theirs. It seemed that their privilege and prestige would forever be accompanied by great consequences.

Chapter 131

July 3, 2012

Morwell, Taggart

Olivia's thoughts were scattered as she completed her walk to work on this overcast Tuesday morning. For the first time since beginning with TI-7, she did not want to go in. It was no longer safe. Not so much in a physical sense, but in terms of normality. What had been predictable and controllable was now unprotected and vulnerable.

She passed through the guard station and swiped her magnetic badge to enter the "cellar." During the night, cleaning teams had apparently come in to remove the mass of broken computer hardware and cables. Technicians were wheeling in boxes of new units on hand trucks as members of the IT staff set up the new terminals. Olivia was surprised by this and spoke to her supervisor, who seemed unusually calm and even cheery.

"What is all of this?" Olivia asked.

"Oh, the usual." Her supervisor smiled and took a sip of her cappuccino. "How are you today?"

Olivia was dumbfounded. It was as if her supervisor had missed the previous day's events and was completely ignorant of the trespass which their unit had suffered. She perceived Olivia's confusion. She set down her cup and studied Olivia's face.

"You are quite the digital soldier, aren't you Olivia? You have taken this to heart more than most, which is why you are so greatly valued on our team."

Olivia's cheeks blushed as she continued. "I know from experience that it can be tempting to wallow in pity or seek retribution in moments like these, but we are professionals. We shall begin again and learn from our mistakes. We will use those lessons to strengthen ourselves so that we may be stronger the next time we suffer an attack."

Olivia realized with dread that something similar could technically happen again next year, tomorrow or even today. The specter of that possibility cast a melancholy shadow across her already downcast outlook.

Olivia gathered herself and asked, "So we are not going to do anything about this? We are going to simply let the perpetrator escape unpunished?"

Her supervisor picked up her cappuccino and took a sip as her suddenly distant gaze indicated that there was some secret knowledge that she had not revealed. "I never said that."

Chapter 132

July 3, 2012

Unknown Location

Spyder was scanning the screens of three different monitors. One displayed the usual stream of data from the programs that were scanning and snooping various networks around the globe. Another screen displayed a bank account, which registered a recent deposit for $15,000.

"Not bad for two week's work," Spyder said aloud.

The third screen displayed multiple computer sites where the latest hardware was listed for sale. Like any tech fashionista, Spyder was determined to keep up with the latest trends.

The face was cast in a strange glow, eyes darting back and forth between the digital offerings when the screens went blank. Spyder frowned, tapped the keyboard and noticed the monitor's power lights were off.

Strange. The battery back-up should have kicked in.

Before any corrective action could be taken, a black cloth bag came down, shutting out the outside world. Strong arms easily lifted the form from the chair and quickly secured his arms with heavy-duty plastic zip ties.

Spyder was too shocked and confused to yell out for help. Perhaps this had been an expected possibility the entire time. In the world of digital espionage, sometimes the spider becomes the prey.

Chapter 133

July 16, 2012

Salmon, Idaho

Two weeks was more than enough time for the reporters and photographers to lose interest and move on to the next news story. The dust had settled and life was resuming its normal rhythm. Thankfully, the rhythm of Joey and Anna's lives was more upbeat and hopeful. Money was still tight, and the roof still needed repair, but a new breeze had blown into their lives. Hope.

Scott and Joey ran into each other at the Elder family's farm. There had been a difficult delivery with a sheep in the middle of the night, some type of predatory animal had broken into the chicken pen, and their workhorse had thrown a shoe. When it rains, it pours.

"How's it going, Hollywood?" Scott asked playfully as he wiped his hands on a towel.

Joey grinned. "I don't see how those celebrities live

like that. Cameras flashin', no privacy. I think I might punch the next guy I find hidin' in my flower bed."

Scott laughed. "Just like ol' Winston. Kind of helps you understand why he went all 'Rocky Balboa' on that guy."

"All they wanted was a break. After hangin' with Grace and Winston, I saw that they are actually just normal folks. They just wanted friends. They just wanted to do something fun. They just wanted to be normal."

Scott processed this as he gathered his instruments and put them into his medical bag. "I still can't believe that you guys are friends with royalty."

"Were," Joey replied curtly.

Scott nodded. "Yeah. That would be a tough relationship to maintain. They're rich. You're a farrier in Salmon, Idaho. They live in a palace in Morwell. You still live in Salmon. They smell nice. You smell like a salmon."

It was a bad joke, but it felt good to kid. It felt good to laugh with a friend.

"I bet that was pretty cool, getting a taste of their lives."

Joey thought back over the last few weeks. "Yeah, it was. I was just so thankful that I could give that to Anna." He paused before ruefully stating, "I wish it hadn't been taken away from her."

Scott listened and nodded sympathetically. "Well, it's not over."

Joey frowned and asked, "What's that supposed to

mean?"

"I'm not really sure. It just came out. But down in my soul, I feel like it's true. You know I don't believe in coincidence. All things happen for a reason. There's a great verse that says 'We know that all things work for good to those who Love God.'"

"I'm not sure I'm in that crowd."

"Maybe you should be. You're healthy. You've got a job. You've got a great wife. You've got that really handsome veterinarian friend. What's his name again?"

"Scott"

"Ah, yes. Scott."

"No, Scott. I'm agreeing with you. I'm seeing all those things in a new light. Ever since I saw Grace in the water and jumped off that cliff, I felt like something was guiding me. It's been the strangest feeling. The hard things, the bad things – I just don't dread 'em like I used to."

Scott looked at his friend and clasped him on the shoulder. "That's fantastic. I'm glad to hear that, Joey. Whatever happens from this point forward, I just want you to remember that it's a process. Trust it. Trust Him."

Joey pondered these things in his heart.

Chapter 134

July 16, 2012

Morwell, Taggart

Winston and Grace collapsed on the bed. They laid back as she kicked off her heels. The last two weeks had been exhausting. There had been endless coverage of the rodeo incident, including horrible nicknames and insinuations. Grace's hair had been returned to its natural color and was regaining some of its length. They looked at each other and smiled.

"Oh, my cheek muscles hurt," she said as she massaged the sides of her jaw. "Being on your best behavior is hard work."

Like grounded teenagers, they had gone over the top trying to get back into the Queen's good graces. They had attended every gala, shook every dignitary's hand and appeared at every press release. The official story had been modified so that the couple had taken an incognito trip to the United States, but that undercover guards had been in place and that not all of the royal's family's affairs are publicized, for security reasons. It wasn't completely untrue and, in some ways, it endeared the couple even more to the public.

"How are you making it, Grace?" Winston asked.

"I'm utterly exhausted," she replied.

His voice became softer. "What I mean is how are you making it without our friends?"

She looked up at the ceiling and thought about it. She had been foolish to think they could have this secret escape from their world. No. They were purebreds who lived on a leash. They did not have the luxury of chasing squirrels and rolling in the dirt. Their place was on the sofa with a perfect serving of gourmet dog food served on a plate of china. But, oh, how they looked out of the window longingly at those free-range beasts.

"I miss them. I miss riding in an old, tattered mini-van with the windows down. I miss the smell of pine, soaking in a hot spring beside a scenic river."

Winston was also looking up at the imaginary screen above which was playing highlights of the last few weeks.

"I miss corn dogs and boots. I miss flying through the air and landing amidst an angry bull and a group of clowns. I don't think I've ever felt more alive."

They laid there in mutual contemplation for several moments. Suddenly, Winston got up and went to the closet, where he began to rummage.

"What on earth are you doing?" she asked.

Suddenly, he turned around, wearing a black Stetson cowboy hat. He had a pencil stuck in mouth, which he pulled out and blew an imaginary cloud of smoke into the air. With a raspy voice and bad Dirty Harry impression, he said, "You ever feel like breakin' the rules, even though you just got in trouble?" He stood there with his right hand near the invisible gun on his hip.

Grace sat up and tried to make sense of this strange version of her husband. It wasn't normal for him – and she liked it. A wide grin crossed her face as she got up, ran to the bathroom vanity and looked through one of the drawers. She returned with an object behind her back. Standing in front of him like a gunslinger, she whipped out the item and held it up in front of her. It was a bottle of blonde hair dye.

John Cleveland

AFTERWORD

I keep asking myself, "Is this a Christian novel?" As I was growing up, many of the offerings in Christian fiction were somewhat lame. Everyone was always blessing each other and speaking in King James. The characters were saintly and nothing was believable.

Rural Royalty is fairly reflective of the world I live in. People, regardless of their station in life, have challenges. They have messy circumstances that they wish they could change. This doesn't mean they're bad people or ungrateful. It simply means that they are going through the human experience.

In your personal circumstances, you may be envying those of another. You may be wishing you could upgrade your spouse, your physique, your bank account or one of a million other transient preferences. As you do, keep in mind that you are the envy of someone else.

To the majority of this planet's population, we are closer to royalty than we are to the commoner. We should not feel guilty for this, but we should use our treasure, time and talent to bless others. Don't feel bad if you've been selfish with these up until now. Instead, join me as we try to push the needle of our generosity further to the other side.

ACKNOWLEDGMENTS

First, giving thanks to God for all things.

Also, I would like to thank the couple that inspired this book. In my eyes, they have demonstrated that powerful, wealthy and influential people can still be kind.

Lastly, to my sweet wife Shanna for being a reason to aim higher, work harder and be better.

ABOUT THE AUTHOR

John Cleveland is an award-winning author known for his first book *40: A Collection of Modern-Day Parables*. After serving in the Army Reserves and retiring from the Highway Patrol, he and his wife moved just west of the Rocky Mountains where they enjoy serving their community and exploring God's creation.

For more information about John Cleveland's work, please visit: www.jcwriting.com

ALSO BY JOHN CLEVELAND

40: A Collection of Modern-Day Parables

Forty short stories about faith, God and human nature. From cruise ships, to electric cars, and even pet dogs, these tales will connect with your heart and soul. Winner of a Christianity Today award.

7: A Sampler from the Larger Collection, "40"

The first seven stories from 40: A Collection of Modern-Day Parables. A small, pocket-sized book that is great to give away as gifts and for events.

The Worst Job Ever (And Why You Should Do It)

A transparent guide for anyone considering a career in law enforcement. It not only covers the basics but gives you an idea of what to expect on patrol and beyond.

Steeped in Shaolin

Imagine if a young American girl were raised by Shaolin Monks. What would that look like when she grows up and returns home to look for her family?

www.ingramcontent.com/pod-product-compliance
Lightning Source LLC
Chambersburg PA
CBHW071145100726
47908CB00002B/253